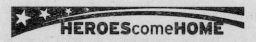

HEROEScomeHOME

A love worth fighting for

They live extraordinary lives on the frontline, but back home they're ordinary men looking for love and family.

Soraya Lane's moving debut will have you crying for all the *right* reasons, so tissues at the ready as our heroes come back to their loved ones—old and new!

Look for Soraya's second heart-wrenching Heroes Come Home story next month:

The Army Ranger's Return

D1469961

Dear Reader,

Soldier on Her Doorstep is truly the book of my heart. From the moment I put pen to paper, Alex and Lisa captured my emotions. All I could think about was the romance between this tortured soldier and a grieving young widow, along with a little girl who needed to find her voice again. I truly believe in the power of love—a man and a woman overcoming their past to embark upon a new future together. But this story is also about the healing power of an animal. Lilly may have lost her father, but she found ongoing comfort from her faithful dog. When all seems lost, there is nothing more special than the love an animal can offer you.

Because this is my debut novel, I want to thank some very important people in my life. My own hero, my wonderful parents, the best writing friend a girl could wish for, a great agent and incredibly talented editors who helped to make this story what it is today.

I hope you enjoy reading *Soldier on Her Doorstep* as much as I enjoyed writing it.

Soraya

SORAYA LANE
Soldier on Her Doorstep

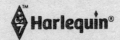

TORONTO NEW YORK LONDON
AMSTERDAM PARIS SYDNEY HAMBURG
STOCKHOLM ATHENS TOKYO MILAN MADRID
PRAGUE WARSAW BUDAPEST AUCKLAND

Recycling programs
for this product may
not exist in your area.

ISBN-13: 978-0-373-17744-8

SOLDIER ON HER DOORSTEP

First North American Publication 2011

Copyright © 2011 by Soraya Lane

Writing romance for Harlequin Mills & Boon is a dream come true for **Soraya Lane**. An avid book reader and writer since her childhood, Soraya describes becoming a published author as "the best job in the world," and hopes to be writing heartwarming, emotional romances for many years to come.

Soraya lives with her own real-life hero on a small farm in New Zealand, surrounded by animals and with an office overlooking a field where their horses graze.

Visit Soraya at www.sorayalane.com.

For my mother, Maureen.

CHAPTER ONE

ALEX DANE didn't need a doctor to tell him his pulse-rate was dangerously high. He pressed two fingers to his wrist and counted, trying to slow his breathing and take hold of the situation.

His heart thudded like a jackhammer hitting Tarmac.

If he didn't have such a strong sense of duty he'd just put the car in gear again.

But he couldn't.

He checked the address on the crumpled scrap of paper before screwing it into a ball again. He knew it by heart, had committed it to memory the day it was passed to him by a dying friend, but still he carried it with him. After all these months it was time to get rid of the paper and fulfill his promise.

Alex dropped his feet out onto the gravel and reached back into the car for the package. His fingers connected with the soft brown paper bag and curled to grasp it. He felt his heart-rate rise again and cursed ever having promised to come here.

It was everything he had expected and yet it wasn't.

The smell of fresh air—of trees, grass and all things country—hit him full force. Smells he had craved when he'd been traipsing across remote deserts in war zones. From where he stood he could only just make out the house, tucked slightly away from the drive, cream weatherboards peeking out from an umbrella of trees that waved above it. It was exactly as William Kennedy had described it.

Alex started to walk. Forced himself to mimic the soldier's beat he knew so well. He swallowed down a gulp of guilt—the same guilt that had plagued him on a daily basis ever since he'd set foot on American soil again—and clenched his hand around the package.

All he had to do was introduce himself, hand over the items, smile, then leave. He just needed to keep that sequence in his head and stick to the plan. No going in for a cup of coffee. No feeling sorry for her. And no looking at the kid.

He found himself at the foot of the porch. Paint peeled off each step, not in a derelict type of way but in a well-loved, haven't quite gotten around to it yet way. A litter of outdoor toys was scattered across the porch, along with a roughed-up rug that he guessed was for a dog.

Alex looked at the door, then down at the bag. If he held it any tighter it might rip. He counted to four, sucked in as much air as his lungs could accommodate, then banged his knuckles in fast succession against the wooden plane of the door.

A scuttle of noise inside told him someone was home. The drum of footsteps fast approaching told him it was time to put the rehearsal into practice. And his mind told him to dump the bag and run like he'd never run before. A damp line of sweat traced along his forehead as he fought to keep his feet rooted to the spot.

He never should have come.

Lisa Kennedy unlocked the door and reached for the handle. She smoothed her other hand over her hair to check her ponytail and pulled the ties on her apron before swinging it open.

A man was standing at the foot of the porch, his back turned as if she'd just caught him walking away. It didn't take a genius to figure out he was a soldier. Not with the short US Army buzz-cut, and that straight, uniformed way he stood, even when he thought no one was watching.

"Can I help you?"

Was he a friend of her late husband's? She had received

plenty of cards and phone calls from men who had been close to him. Was this another, come to pay his respects after all these months?

The man turned. A slow swivel on the spot before facing her front-on. Lisa played with the string of her apron, her interest piqued. The blond buzz-cut belonged to a man with the deepest brown eyes she'd ever seen, shoulders the breadth of a football player's, and the saddest smile a man could own. The woman in her wanted to hold him, to ask this soldier what he'd seen that had made him so sad. But the other part of her, the part that knew what it was to be a soldier's wife, knew that war was something he might not want to recall. Not with a face that haunted. Not when sadness was raining from his skin.

"Lisa Kennedy?"

She almost dropped the apron then. Hearing her name from his lips made her feel out of breath—winded, almost.

"I'm sorry, do I know you?"

He closed the gap between them, slowly walking up the two steps until he was standing only a few feet away.

"I was a friend of your husband's." His voice was strained.

She smiled. So that was why he'd been walking away. She knew how hard it was for soldiers to confront what another man had lost. She guessed this guy had been serving in the same unit as William and must have just been shipped home.

"It's kind of you to come by."

Lisa reached out to touch his arm, her fingers only just skimming his skin before he pulled away. He jumped like she'd touched him with a lick of fire. Recoiled like he'd never felt a woman's touch before.

She slowly took back her hand and folded her arms instead. He was hurting, and clearly not used to contact. Lisa decided to approach him as the stranger he was. A wave of uncertainty tickled her shoulders, but she shrugged it away. The man was nervous, but if he'd served with William she had to trust him.

Now that she'd had longer to study him, she realized how

handsome he'd be if only he knew how to smile, to laugh. Unlike her husband—who had had deep laugh lines etched into his skin, and a face so open that every thought he'd had was there for all to see—this man was a blank canvas. Strong cheekbones, thick cropped hair, and skin the color of a drizzle of gold, tanned from hours out in the open.

She put his quietness down to being shy—nervous, perhaps.

"Would you like to come in? I could do with an iced tea," she offered.

She watched as he searched to find the right words. It was sad. A man so handsome, so strong, and yet so clearly struggling to make a start again as a civilian.

"I... Ah..." he cleared his throat and shifted on the spot.

Lisa felt a tug at the leg of her jeans and instinctively reached for her daughter. Lilly hadn't spoken a word to anyone but Lisa since she'd been told that Daddy wouldn't be coming home, and clung on to her mother at times like she never wanted to let go.

The look on the man's face was transformed into something resembling fear, and Lisa had a feeling he wasn't used to children. Seeing Lilly had certainly unnerved him. Made him look even sadder, more tortured than before, if that were possible.

"Lilly, you go find Boston," she said, fluffing her daughter's long hair. "There's a bone in the fridge he might like. You can reach it."

Lisa looked over at the man again, who had clearly lost his tongue, and decided that if he was used to orders then that was what she'd give him. A firm instruction and a knowing look.

"Soldier, you sit there," she instructed, pointing toward the big old swinging chair on the porch. "I'm going to fix us something to drink and you can tell me exactly what you're doing here in Brownswood, Alaska."

Something flashed across his face, something she thought might be guilt, but she ignored it. He moved to the seat.

Lisa stifled a smile. When was it that you became your own mother? She was sounding more like hers every day.

This man meant her no harm, she was sure. He was probably suffering something like shell-shock, and nervous about turning up on her doorstep, but she could handle it.

Besides, it wasn't every day a handsome man turned up looking for her. Even if it was only sharing a glass of tea with a guy who didn't have a lot to say, she wouldn't mind the company.

And he'd obviously come with a purpose. Why else would she have found him on her doorstep?

Alex summoned every descriptive word for an idiot he could and internally yelled them. He had stood there like a fool, gaping at the poor woman, while she'd looked back and probably wondered what loony hospital he'd come from.

What had happened to the sequence? To the plan? He looked down at the paper bag on the seat beside him and cursed it. Just like he'd done when he'd first held it in his hands.

William had said a lot about his wife. About the type of person she was, about how he loved her, and about what a great mom she was. But he had sure never said how attractive she was.

He didn't know why, but it made the guilt crawl further, all over his skin. He'd had a certain profile of her in his mind. And it wasn't anything like the reality.

Maybe it was the long hair. The thick chestnut mane that curled gently into a ponytail. The deep hazel eyes framed by decadent black lashes. Or the way her jeans hugged her frame and the tank top showed more female skin than he'd seen in a long time. A very long time.

Then again, the fact that she was minus the pregnant belly he'd been expecting might have altered his mindset too. Would he have even noticed her figure if he hadn't been searching for the baby? Alex knew the answer to that question. Any man would. Lisa was beautiful, in a fresh-faced, innocent kind of way, and he'd have to be cold-blooded not to notice.

So had she lied to her husband about the baby she was expecting? Or had Alex lost track of time and the baby was already born?

Alex went through the plan in his mind and cursed ever coming here. He hadn't introduced himself. He hadn't smiled. And he hadn't passed her the bag or refused to stay.

His assessment? He was a complete dunce. And if the kid had any instincts whatsoever she'd probably be scared of him too. He'd looked at her as if she was an exotic animal destined to kill him.

When he'd been deployed it had been all about the plan. He had never strayed from it. Ever.

Here, one pretty woman and a cute kid had rendered him incapable of even uttering a single word.

Or perhaps it was glimpsing family life that had tied him in knots. The kind of life he'd done his best to avoid.

Alex looked up as he heard a soft thump of footfalls on the porch. He took a deep breath and made himself smile. It was something he was going to have to learn to do again. To just smile for the hell of it. Sounded easy, but for some reason he found it incredibly hard these days.

But he needn't have bothered. The only being watching him was of the four-legged variety, and he beat Alex in the smile stakes hands down. He found himself staring into the face of a waggy-tailed golden retriever, with a smile so big he could see every tooth the canine owned. He guessed this was Boston.

"Hey, bud," he said.

As he spoke he realized how stupid he must sound. He had been tongue-tied around Lisa, yet here he was talking to her dog.

Boston seemed to appreciate the conversation. He extended one paw and waved it, flapping it around in midair. Did he want Alex to shake it?

"Well, I'm pleased to meet you too, I guess."

A noise behind him made Alex stop, his hand less than an inch from taking Boston's paw. Lisa was walking out with a tray. He pretended not to notice the flicker of a smile she tried to hide. At least he was providing her with some afternoon entertainment.

She placed the pitcher of iced tea and a plate of cookies on the table in front of him.

If he'd felt like an idiot before, now he felt like the class clown.

"I see you've met Boston," she commented.

Alex nodded, a slow movement of his head. How long had she been standing there?

"He's well trained," he finally said.

Lisa laughed. It caught Alex by surprise. It seemed like forever since he'd heard the soft tinkle of a woman's happiness.

"Lilly likes to teach him tricks. You could say he's a very fast learner." She tossed the dog a broken piece of cookie. "Especially when there's food involved."

They sat there for a moment in silence. Alex fought for the words he wanted to say. The bag seemed to be staring at him. Pulsating as if it had a heart. He knew he could only make small talk for so long until he had to tell her. It had been eating away at him for months now. He had to get it out.

She pulled over a beaten-up-looking chair and sat down in it. He watched as she poured them each a glass of tea.

"I'm guessing you served with my husband?"

He had been expecting the question but still it hit him. Gave him an ache in his shoulders that was hard to shrug.

Alex allowed himself a moment to catch his words. Talking had never really been his thing.

"Lisa." He waited until she was sitting back in her chair, nursing the tea. "When your husband returned from leave, we were assigned to work together again."

He fought to keep his eyes on hers, but found it was easier to flit between the pitcher and her face. She was so beautiful, so heartbreakingly beautiful, in a soft, unassuming way, and it made it harder to tell her. He didn't want to see the kind features of her face crumple as he described the end. Didn't know if he could bear seeing this woman cry. Seeing those cracked hazelnut eyes fill with tears.

"We became very close during that tour, and he told me a lot about you. About Lilly too."

"Go on," she said, leaning forward.

"Lisa, I was there with him when he died." He said those words fast, racing to get them out. "He passed away very quickly, and I was there with him until the end." He eliminated the part about how the bullet should have been for him. How William had been so intent on warning Alex, on getting him out of harm's way, that he had been shot in the process. *Always putting his men first.* That was what the army had said about him. And it was a statement Alex knew first-hand to be true.

He looked back at Lisa. He had expected tears—uncontrollable sobbing, even—but she looked calm. Her smile was now sad, but the anguish he had worried about wasn't there.

Her quiet helped him to catch his breath and conjure the words he'd practiced for so long.

"Before he died, he scrawled down your address. Told me that I had to come here and see you, to check on you, and to tell you that…"

Lisa moved from her seat to the swinging chair, her body landing close to his. He could feel her weight on the cushion, feel the heat of her so close to him. This time when she reached for him he didn't pull away. Couldn't.

He turned to face her.

"He told me to tell you that he loved you and Lilly. That you were the woman he always dreamed of."

Now she did have tears in her eyes. A flood of wetness threatening to spill, overflowing against her lashes. She gave him a small, tremulous smile.

"He said that he wanted you to be happy," Alex finished.

Alex felt a weight lift as he said the words—words that had echoed in his head from the moment he had been told them— as if he had been scared that he might forget them. Words that had haunted him.

"Typical," she said, tucking one foot beneath her as she dabbed at her eyes with the back of one finger. Her other hand left his arm. He could feel the heat of where it had been. "He goes and leaves me, then tells me he wants me to be happy."

Alex looked away. He didn't know what comfort he could offer.

Then his fingers touched the bag.

"I have some things of his," he said. "Here." He passed it to her and another feeling of relief hit him. It felt so good to finally pass it on to her. The guilt would have eaten him alive had he not gone through with this. And he didn't need any more guilt to live with. He was carrying enough already.

He felt her sit up straighter.

"What's in here?"

"Some letters, a photo of Lilly, and his old tags."

"He asked you to give these to me?" she pressed.

Alex nodded.

"Have you read them?" she asked, her fingers already clasped around the cluster of papers inside.

"No, ma'am."

She slipped them back into the bag and leaned forward to place it on the table.

"My husband trusted you to come here, to visit me, and I don't even know your name," she said lightly.

Alex stood.

"Alex Dane," he said, arms hanging awkwardly at his sides.

"Alex," she repeated.

The smile she gave him made him want to run. Even more so than earlier, when she'd opened the door. This woman was supposed to be grieving—unhappy, miserable, even. Not kind and smiling. Not ponytail-swishingly beautiful.

He had been prepared for sadness and she'd thrown him.

"Thank you for the tea, but I'd better get on my way," he announced abruptly.

"Oh, no, you don't," she said.

He grimaced as she grabbed a hold of his wrist, but didn't let himself resist.

"You're staying for dinner and I won't take no for an answer."

He let himself be frog-marched toward the front door and fought not to pull away from her.

He should never have come.

A set of blue eyes peeking out from beneath a blonde fringe watched him from the end of the hallway. The smell of baking filled his nostrils. A framed photo of William smiled down at him from the wall.

He was in another man's house. With another man's wife and another man's child. He had stepped into someone else's life and it wasn't right.

But, even though he knew it was wrong, he felt strangely like he'd arrived home.

Not that he should know what a home felt like.

Lisa filled the kettle and set it to boil. Despite his odd behavior, she felt at ease with Alex in her home. It wasn't like she had a lack of visitors—ever since she'd heard the news of William's passing she'd had family and friends constantly dropping by. Not to mention her sister, acting as if she was a child needing tender care. It seemed she always had an excuse to drop past.

And she'd had plenty of soldiers visit. Just not for a while now.

She glanced over at Alex. He was sitting only a few feet from her, yet he could have been on the other side of the State. There was a closed expression on his face, and she was certain he was unaware of it. From what she'd read about returned soldiers there were many who never recovered from what they'd seen at war. Others just needed time, though, and she hoped this was the case with Alex. She could feel that he needed help.

Part of her was just plain curious about him. The other more demanding side of her wanted to interrogate him about William's death, and about what it was that troubled him. She guessed she had some time to ask questions, but how much could she ask him over one afternoon and dinner?

"Do you take sugar?"

She watched as he looked up at her, his gaze still uncertain.

"One sugar. Thank you."

She spooned coffee granules into each cup, added sugar, then poured the now boiled water. Lisa could feel him watching her, but she didn't mind. There was something oddly comforting about knowing that he'd been with William at the end.

She cleared her throat before turning around and passing him his coffee. She noticed that his eyes danced over her body, but she had the feeling he wasn't checking her out. It was more as if he was making an assessment of her, looking for something.

"I don't have a handgun on me, if that's what you're worried about." She laughed at herself, but he didn't even crack a smile. Instead his face turned a burnished red. She felt an unfamiliar flutter herself. Maybe she'd been out of the game for so long she didn't even know when a man *was* checking her out! It felt weird. Not uncomfortable, but not exactly something she was ready for. Although now she'd obviously made *him* uncomfortable. "I'm sorry, Alex. I was joking."

He looked away. "I'm just confused, that's all."

She raised an eyebrow in question.

Alex sighed and clasped the hot mug.

"William mentioned you were expecting another baby."

Uh-huh. The penny dropped. She almost felt disappointed that Alex *hadn't* been sizing her up, but then she guessed it wasn't really appropriate for a widow to get excited about another man anyway. It was just that she hadn't seen her husband for such a long time, and it had been months since his passing, and she...wanted to feel like a woman again. Not just a widow, or a mother, or a wife. Like a woman.

It didn't mean she didn't love her husband. She did. She had. So much. She blinked the confusion away and smiled reassuringly at Alex, knowing how uncomfortable he must be, saying something like that. It wasn't like she owed him an explanation, but the guy had traveled from heaven only knew where to visit her, to fulfill some dying wish of William's, and she didn't mind sharing. Not if it gave him some peace of mind before he left and went back to his own family.

"I fell pregnant when William was home on leave. I had an inkling and took an early test the day before he left."

Alex was still blushing. She guessed he wasn't used to talking pregnancy and babies with another man's wife. But he'd asked.

"I lost the baby during my first trimester, but I couldn't quite figure out how to tell William. He was so excited that we were finally having a second child, and he was unsure about being away again. I didn't want to let him down. But then he died, so he never knew." Lisa paused. "If I hadn't lost the baby it would have been born a couple of months ago."

She took a sip of coffee and then gazed into the liquid black depths of it. It was still hard talking about William, knowing he wasn't ever going to be coming back, but she was dealing with it. She felt like the deepest grieving was over, but sometimes it was still hard. Sometimes the sadness was...trying.

"Sorry. Time kind of gets away from you when you're away," he said.

Lisa nodded.

"Were you right in not telling him what had happened to the baby?" he asked.

Alex's question surprised her. He wasn't accusing her. Nor offering an opinion. It seemed he was just asking it the way he saw it.

"Yeah, I think so." Her voice sounded weak even to her own ears. "I'm glad he died thinking that I was going to have a baby to love. That Lilly would have a brother or sister."

She hadn't talked about her miscarriage to anyone, really. Not even her mother. It felt good to get it out, especially to someone who wouldn't make a fuss or make the pain of it come back to her.

Alex didn't respond. He'd wanted to know but she guessed he hadn't banked on hearing that.

"I'm sorry. I mean, I'm just…"

"Not sure what to say?" she finished for him, trying to put him at ease.

"Yeah."

She nodded. Her usual response would be to touch, to reach for the person she was talking to. But she stopped herself. Alex wasn't her usual company, and she needed to give him space.

"Would you like something to eat?"

He shook his head. "No, don't go to any trouble."

Lisa rolled her eyes at him, getting used to his short answers and lack of expression. "I write cookbooks for a living. Believe me when I say that fixing you something to eat is not going to put me in a tailspin."

She placed her hands on the bench and caught a smile on Alex's face. Not a big smile, just a gentle curling of his lips at each corner and a dance of something she hadn't seen in his eyes earlier. A lightness that had been missing before.

"You'll have to battle it out with Lilly, though. That girl eats like a horse," she said wryly.

Alex chuckled. A deep, sexy baritone kind of a chuckle that finally made Lisa feel like they were having an adult, woman-to-man kind of conversation.

"I'm hungry, but I don't think she'll be much competition."

They grinned at one another and Lisa hollered for her daughter.

"Lilly! Time for a snack."

A cacophony of feet on timber echoed down the hallway. She watched as first Lilly appeared, then Boston, his tongue hanging out the side of his mouth. They were inseparable, those two. Best friends.

She placed a glass of milk on the counter to keep her daughter busy while she dished out the goodies.

"Would you like to say hello to our guest?"

Lisa knew it was highly unlikely, but the therapist had said to act like everything was normal. To ignore her not talking and just behave as usual—as if she was still speaking to people besides her mother and the dog.

Lilly shook her head, but she wasn't as shy as she'd been. She climbed up onto the third stool, leaving the one in the middle empty, her eyes wide and fixed on Alex.

"This is Alex," Lisa told her. "He was a friend of Daddy's."

That made Lilly look harder at him. Her big eyes searched his face intently.

Lilly smiled and gave him a little wave.

"Hi," he said.

Lisa was more shocked at hearing Alex talk, albeit monosyllabically, than if Lilly had spoken! "Alex is a soldier," she explained.

Lisa glanced at Alex and saw how uncomfortable he looked at being so thoroughly inspected by a child. Back straight, pupils dilated, body tense. She guessed if you weren't used to the curiosity of a child it might come as a surprise. Did he not have a family?

She left them both looking at one another and opened up the pantry. Lilly would guzzle that milk in no time and start wriggling for something to eat. Everything was neatly stacked before her—jars and containers filled with all sorts of goodies. She made Lilly eat plenty of fruit and vegetables at other times, but a mid-afternoon snack was their one daily indulgence and she loved it. Lisa reached for her homemade brownies and iced lemon cake, putting the containers within reach and placing an array of each on a big square white plate.

"I hope you have a sweet tooth, Alex. This will have to do for the meantime."

He still looked like a nocturnal animal caught within the web of a bright light, but she ignored it.

"Are you planning on staying in the area?" She pushed a plate of baking toward him.

"Ah...depends on what the fishing is like. I hear it's pretty good," he said awkwardly.

"You're a fisherman, then?"

She watched as he finished his mouthful, Adam's apple bobbing up and down.

"I just like to look out at a lake and fish. You know—take time out. It's more about the sitting and thinking than serious fishing," he acknowledged.

Oh, she knew. It was exactly why they'd bought this house in the first place. Was he camping out alone? After being away on tour she'd have expected he'd want to be with his family. With friends.

Lisa moved away to locate some napkins and stopped for a heartbeat to look out the big kitchen window. The water seemed to lull her, made her feel like anything was possible as she briefly stared into its depths. She'd never really liked fishing, but she loved to think, to just sit and stare at the water. When she'd heard the dreadful news that her husband had died, that was exactly what she'd done. For hours every day.

Lilly tugged at her arm. She hadn't even seen her slip off the stool. Lisa bent down so Lilly could cup her hand around her ear.

"Tell him we have lots of fish to catch."

She smiled and nodded at her daughter.

"Tell him," Lilly insisted.

The little girl hopped back on her stool and smiled at Alex. He looked confused.

"Lilly wants me to tell you we have lots of fish here."

"Fish?"

Lilly nodded while licking at her fingers, devouring what was left of the brownie. Then she reached, slowly, for Alex's hand. She gave it a tap and jumped down.

Alex looked from Lilly to her.

"I...ah...think she wants you to go with her. To the lake."

Lisa held her breath as Lilly stood, looking expectantly up at Alex. If she didn't know better, she'd have thought his hands were shaking. He didn't move, his eyes flitting between her and her daughter, but then slowly he shifted his feet and drew himself up to his full height. He towered above Lilly. Like a bear beside a bird.

"Okay," he said uncertainly.

Lilly reached for his hand and tugged him along, and all Alex could do was obey. He looked like a placid cattle beast being led off to slaughter, but Lisa wasn't going to step in and save him.

It was the first time Lilly had interacted with a stranger in a long while. Lisa didn't care how uncomfortable their guest was. This was a major turning point. Lilly hadn't spoken to him, but she'd definitely wanted to communicate.

There was no way she was going to intervene. She couldn't.

Lisa nodded at Boston to go with them, then held her breath. Alex was either going to bolt at the first chance or respond to Lilly, and for both their sakes she hoped it was the latter.

He was a stranger, so she knew how odd it was, but deep down she hoped he *would* stay for dinner. So they could talk about William. About the war. She felt a bond with him, knowing that he'd probably spent more time with William than she had in the past couple of years. It was an opportunity she didn't want to miss.

Besides, although she'd never admitted it to her family, she was kind of lonely. At nights, mainly. She always had been, but at least she'd known one day it would be a house she would share full-time with William. That one day in the future she would have him home every night for dinner.

Lisa put down her coffee with a shaky hand and decided to change her mind and follow them after all. It wasn't that she didn't trust this Alex with her daughter, she just wanted to make sure it wasn't too much for Lilly. Or for Alex.

Right now she was Lilly's chief interpreter. And besides, she was curious to see how this unlikely pair were going to get along down by the lake.

CHAPTER TWO

"HAS Lilly always been quiet?"

Alex glanced at Lisa as they turned back toward the house. They'd been walking along the river, back and forth, Alex throwing a stick out into the water, Lilly clapping her hands and wrestling it back from Boston the moment he retrieved it.

It wasn't like he'd asked Lilly much when they were alone—he didn't even know what to say to a child—but she seemed very quiet for a little girl.

"She's been virtually mute with everyone but me since William died."

Alex nodded thoughtfully. "How old is she?"

"Six."

He'd wanted to know whether the little girl was able to speak or not, but he didn't want to talk about it. He knew what it was like to have a rough time as a kid, and it wasn't a place he wanted to go back to, even in talking about someone else. When he'd joined the army he'd tried to leave all those memories, those thoughts from his past behind.

"She's having a good day today, though. I thought she'd be too shy to be around you but she's not at all," Lisa said.

Alex liked that the girl wasn't afraid of him, but he didn't want to get involved. Didn't want to bond with anyone. Not even the dog.

"Boston seems pretty protective of her," he commented.

That made Lisa laugh. He wanted to jump back, to walk away from her. It all seemed too real, too normal, to just be talking like this after so long thinking, wondering how he was going to cope seeing her, and now to hear her laugh like that…

"That dog is her best friend. I don't know what we would have done without him. Worth his weight in gold," she told him.

They kept walking. Alex didn't know what to say. Part of him wanted to get in the car and drive—anywhere, fast, just to get away—but the other part of him, the part he didn't want to give in to, wanted to stay. To be part of this little family for a few hours, to see what William had lost, to know what his friend had sacrificed to let *him* live.

"Come on, Lil, let's go back inside."

She came running when her mother called, but Alex knew deep down that her being so quiet wasn't right. He hadn't exactly had much experience with children, but he knew that she should be squealing when the dog shook water on her, yelling back to her mother when she called. Instead she smiled quietly, not obviously sad or grieving, but obviously mourning her father in her own silent way.

He wished he didn't know what she was going through, but he did.

The army had been his only family for years. It had been the source of all his friendships, the place where he had a home, his support.

So he knew exactly how alone a person could feel.

Lisa rummaged in the fridge to find the ingredients she needed. It was going to be an early dinner. The only way she had been able to relieve Alex from being Lilly's sidekick was to order them both inside because it was almost dinnertime. Now she had to rustle something up. Fast.

She thought about the times William had returned from duty. He'd always been ravenous for a home-cooked meal. Hadn't often minded what it was, so long as it resembled comfort food. The type they missed out on over there in the desert.

"How long were you on tour this time, Alex?" she queried.

He was back sitting on the bar stool, casually flicking through one of her older cookbooks. He looked up. She could see a steely glint in his eye. Got the feeling it was a back-off-and-don't-talk-about-the-war kind of look emerging.

"Months. I kind of lost count," he finally admitted.

She didn't believe it for a second. Her husband had always known exactly how many days he'd spent away each time. Had probably been able to work out the hours he'd been away from home after each tour if he'd had a mind to.

"You been back awhile, or fresh off the plane?"

There he went with that look again. "About a week."

It was like a wall had closed, been built over his eyes, over his face, as soon as she'd started talking about the army. She could take a hint. There was no reason to pry.

"Well, I'll bet you're hankering for a nice home-cooked meal, then."

He nodded. Politely. She was desperate to ask him more. Why he wasn't sitting right now with his own family having a meal. What had made him come here to visit her so soon after he'd arrived home.

She wondered at how he and William had gotten on. They were so different. Alex was quiet and guarded—or maybe that was just a reaction to her questions. Her husband had been open and talkative. Forward.

But she knew from all the stories he'd told her that it was different at war. That men you might never have made friends with, men you ended up serving with, became as close to you as a brother. She hoped it had been that way with Alex and him.

She began peeling. Potatoes first, then carrots.

"I think what you need is Shepherd's Chicken Pie."

He smiled. A half-smile, but more open than before.

"Want to give me a hand?"

He nodded. "Sure."

"Would you mind slicing those potatoes for me? Knife's just in the drawer there. And then put them in the pot to boil."

Alex slipped down off the chair and moved to join her. She should have suggested it all along. Even if he wasn't sure what to do, keeping him busy and not interrogating him was probably the best way to help him relax and eventually open up a little about William.

She was desperate to hear some stories. If only the task didn't feel quite so similar to drawing blood from a stone!

"When you're finished there you can take over the dicing here, and I'll pop out back to pick some herbs," she instructed.

His arm moved slowly back and forth, his other hand holding the vegetables in place as he cut them. She'd never thought about it before, but the way a person cooked, prepared food, showed a lot. Her, she made a mess and enjoyed herself, when it came to family cooking especially, but Alex was meticulous. He sliced each ingredient with military precision. If she stepped closer, she'd bet she'd see that every piece of carrot was diced to exactly the same dimensions.

He was a soldier. The way he moved, held himself and carried out tasks, marked him as army. It comforted her.

William had been similar in many ways. Not exactly like Alex, but the soldier aspects still made her think of him.

"You all right there for a moment?" she asked him.

He stopped slicing and looked at her. She could see a softness in his gaze now, a change that showed her she'd been right to just give him a task and leave him be.

"Sure."

Lisa served the pie. The potato top was slightly browned, the gravy running out over the spoon as she manhandled it into three bowls.

"Lilly, why don't you take yours into the TV room? You can watch a DVD."

Her daughter nodded eagerly. Lisa hardly ever let her eat away from the table, but tonight she wanted the luxury of chatting openly to their guest.

Lisa passed her a smaller bowlful, and then set the other two on the table.

"I really can't thank you enough, Alex. For coming here to see me."

He quickly forked some pie into his mouth—so he didn't have to answer her, she guessed wryly.

"I've had plenty of soldiers drop by, but none for a few months. Still the odd call sometimes—to check up on me, I guess—but not many house calls." She paused, but he didn't respond. She tried again. "William didn't often tell me the names of his soldier friends. Well, he called them by their last names, so I kind of got lost."

"Yeah, that's army for you," he muttered.

She took a mouthful of dinner herself, and gave him time to finish some more of his.

"The time you spent together—did you…ah…get along well?" she pressed cautiously.

His lips formed a tight line. His face was serious, eyebrows drawn together. His entire body rigid. She'd pushed him too far, too soon.

"Ma'am, I…" He stopped and took a breath. "I'm not really one for talking about what happened over there."

She felt embarrassed. She should have known better. It was just that she felt like they only had a few hours together and she wanted to hear everything. Was curious to find out more.

"I'm sorry, Alex. Listen to me—interrogating you when you've come here out of kindness," she apologized.

He put down his fork. "I don't mean to be rude, I just…"

"I understand. My husband was a talker—he liked getting everything off his chest," she explained.

They both went back to eating. The silence that was suspended between them felt knife-edged.

* * *

He knew she wanted him to open up, but he couldn't. It just wasn't him. And what could he say? *Yeah, William and I got on real well while we knew each other. Before he took a bullet intended for me. Before he died trying to save me.*

The food was great. He did appreciate it. But she was treating him like the good guy here. What would she think if she could actually see what had happened over there? Could watch it like a movie before her eyes and see William dive into the line of fire to cover *him*?

He forced more food down. Anything to put the memories back on hold.

"Where's home, Alex? Where do your family live?" she asked.

Alex felt a shudder trawl his backbone. He fought the tic in his cheek as he clamped his jaw tightly. He didn't want to talk about his family. Or lack of. He didn't want to talk about why he didn't have a home. "I don't have a place at the moment," he bit out tersely.

"But what about your family? They must be excited to have you back?"

He shook his head.

Lisa watched him, her eyes questioning, but to his relief she didn't ask again. He didn't want to be rude, but there were some things he just didn't want to talk about.

She didn't need to know he was an orphan. He didn't need any sympathy, pity. Lisa was best not knowing.

"Well, I'm glad we were able to have you for dinner," she said after a long pause.

"I promised William I'd find you." He looked up, braved her gaze. "I set out as soon as I was debriefed."

She nodded. "Well, I certainly appreciate you coming here."

"Great food, by the way. Really good," he said stiltedly.

It didn't come easy to him. Just chatting. Making small talk. But he didn't want to get on the topic of family again, and she was making a real effort for him. It wasn't that he didn't appreciate it, he just wanted to keep certain doors firmly closed.

"I'm going to check on Lilly. Help yourself to more," she offered.

Lisa pulled the door to Lilly's room almost shut, leaving it so a trickle of light still traced into the room, and wiggled her fingers at her. She'd read her a story, kissed her good-night, then turned the light out.

She heard Alex down in the kitchen. He might have been in the army for years and be as quiet as a mouse, but he was well trained. He'd cleared the table and started the dishes all before she'd scooted Lilly upstairs to bed.

"You don't need to do that." She swallowed her words as soon as she saw the kitchen. The counter had been wiped down, the dishwasher light was on, and the sink was empty. He'd even fed the dog the leftovers.

He shrugged. "It's the least I can do."

She didn't know about that. He'd traipsed from goodness-only-knew-where to get here, brought things to her that meant the world, and started to cheer up a six-year-old who was undergoing serious counseling for trauma. Lilly had been happy and bubbling when Lisa had marched her up to bed.

"Alex—stay the night. Please. It's too late for you to find somewhere in town," she said.

He looked uncomfortable. She wished he didn't. A frown shadowed his face. Whatever it was that was troubling him was firmly locked away. She'd seen it written on his face tonight at the table.

"I really appreciate the offer, but you've already cooked me dinner and…"

"Don't be silly."

The man seemed to have no family. Or none that he wanted to talk about. No place to go nearby anyway. She wasn't exactly going to turf him out. Not after what he'd done for her. Not when he'd been the man to give William comfort as he died.

"Lisa, I didn't come here expecting accommodation," he said abruptly.

She put her hands on her hips. "No, you came from miles away to do something nice for a stranger. It's me who feels like I owe you."

He had that awkward look again. On his face, in the angles of his arms as they hung by his sides. He looked up at the clock on the wall. It was getting late. "Are you sure? I can pitch my tent out back."

Lisa laughed. "Oh, no, you won't. Come on—I'll show you the guestroom."

Alex hesitated. "I've got my camping gear..."

"Don't be silly. The bed is made. You can get a good night's sleep. Come on," she said firmly.

He didn't look entirely comfortable about the situation, but he didn't argue. She smiled.

Resigned acceptance traced across his face. "I'll...ah...just grab my things from the car."

Lisa went to flick the switch on the kettle. She reached for an oversize mug and stirred in some of her homemade chocolate.

By the time he reappeared, duffle bag slung over his shoulder, she had a steaming mug of hot chocolate waiting for him.

"This is for you," she said, passing the cup to him before walking off.

She led the way up the stairs. She didn't turn, but she could hear him following. The treads creaked and groaned under his weight, as they had done under hers. She led him to the third bedroom and stepped aside so he could enter.

His big frame seemed to fill the entire room. The spare bed looked too small for him. She stifled a laugh. He looked like a grown-up in a playhouse.

"Just call if you need anything. Bathroom's the last room down the hall."

He nodded.

"Well, good night then," she said.

"Night," he replied.

Lisa pulled the door shut behind him. And walked away.

The image of him standing forlorn, bag over one shoulder and hot chocolate in hand, stayed with her, though.

She went back down the stairs, careful to avoid the noisy steps, and flicked off the lights. She reached to switch on a lamp instead.

The paper bag Alex had given her rested on the side table. Her fingers took ownership of it. Lisa found herself wondering whether the bag had come with Alex from war or if it was something he had put the items in after he'd arrived home.

She tipped out the contents. A crinkled photo of Lilly fell on to her lap. Lisa retrieved it and held it up to the light. Lilly was maybe four years old in the shot. Her blonde hair was caught into a tiny ponytail, and she was sitting on the grass.

Lisa remembered the day well. William had been between postings. They'd had an entire summer together—probably the best summer of her life. Lilly had been entertaining them right up until that moment, when she'd gotten a bee sting.

It had been William she'd run to for comfort. It always had been when he'd been home. Like she wanted to spend as much time with her daddy before he left as possible.

Lisa put the photo back on the table. She reached for William's tags this time, and slung them around her neck. The cool hit of metal chilled her chest, but she didn't remove them. Instead she let her left hand hover over them. Feeling him. Remembering him. Loving him.

Then she took the letters out. There were three of them in total. She guessed he had been waiting for an opportunity to send them.

Her heart skipped when she unfolded the first one. Saw his neat, precise writing as it filled the page.

To my darling wife.

He'd always started his letters the same way. He hadn't been one of those soldier husbands who'd been macho and brave with his family. He'd always told her he loved her on the phone, whenever he'd been able to call, regardless of how many men surrounded him. They'd always been close.

Lisa bit the inside of her lip as a wave of tears threatened. Her bottom lip started to quiver and she pushed her teeth in harder. But every word she read, every sentence that pulled her into his letter, made more tears form, until they rained a steady beat on her cheeks.

She could taste them as the salty wetness fell, trickling into her mouth.

William had died months ago, and in the year before that she'd only seen him once—the six weeks he'd spent at home on leave.

But when she read the words he had so lovingly penned for her it made her feel as if they'd never spent any time apart at all. As if he was in the room, his warm body tucked behind her on the sofa, whispering the words in her ear.

They'd been best friends, her and William. Friends before they'd become lovers.

They were friends first—that was what they'd always said to one another. Friends because they would do anything for one another, comfort one another and support one another through anything. Friends because they didn't want to hold one another back or stop the other from doing what they wanted.

And as his friend she had a strange feeling that he wouldn't be nearly as upset about the tiny flare of attraction she had briefly—very briefly—felt for the man staying upstairs as most deceased husbands would. He was so different from William, but Alex reminded her in so many ways of him. Made her pine for her husband all over again.

William had always said to her, every time he'd left to go back offshore, that if anything ever happened to him she was to move on and be happy. That she wasn't to grieve and stay in a black hole of sadness.

It wasn't that she wanted to move on. Not yet. Not at all. She just didn't want to feel guilty for being mildly attracted to another man. A flicker of attraction, nothing more, but still something she had wanted to chastise herself for at the time.

With Alex upstairs, she didn't want to feel unfaithful to William. Because she *had* felt a stirring within herself. She couldn't lie. There was no denying it. He had made a tiny beat pound inside her chest.

He was a troubled soldier. She was a widow.

But it didn't mean she couldn't appreciate that he was an attractive man.

Was it right that she'd asked him to stay the night? She hoped so. From his lack of response earlier, it was obvious he didn't have anywhere else to go.

And she'd never turn a friend of William's away.

CHAPTER THREE

LISA watched through the window as Lilly tripped along the lakefront, looking over her shoulder every few steps to check that Alex was following. The child had dragged him outside as soon as they'd finished breakfast, and he'd been forced to accompany her. She wasn't talking to him, but her expressions said a million words. Boston trotted along behind, his nose tipped to sniff the air.

Lisa moved away to put her coffee mug in the sink, and stopped for a heartbeat to look out the other, larger kitchen window. The water twinkled at her, comforted her. Then a tree, waving, caught her eye. Made her glance at the little cottage only just visible.

She tried not to smile.

That was it!

She had always believed in destiny, and as the cottage peeked back at her an idea hit her.

It was the perfect solution.

It would give Alex time to fish, and she could get to know the man who had seen her husband gulp his last breath and try to help him.

She looked at the cottage again. When they'd first moved here they'd talked about doing all sorts of things to it. Turning it into guest accommodation…making it into a studio for her to write in. But in the end having strangers to stay for a bit of extra money had worried her more than anything, and the last thing she'd want would be to work on her recipe books away from the kitchen.

The last time William was home they'd had a poke around out there. Dumped some old boxes and wiped some cobwebs away. Then they'd decided it would be for Lilly—as a playhouse while she was young, and as a teenage retreat for when she was older.

They had called it a cottage, but it wasn't really worthy of the name. Maybe a cabin was more fitting? There was one large room that doubled as the living and sleeping quarters, plus an old bathroom and a measly kitchenette.

Alex caught her eye. He glanced into the house at her. She raised a hand in a wave. He didn't smile back, but she saw recognition in his eyes. Like he was reaching out to her.

He was afraid.

She decided to go out and rescue him.

She was no therapist, but she could tell when people needed healing, and Alex Dane needed a lot of rest and recovery.

So did Lilly.

Lisa just had to convince him to stay.

Alex felt lost. It wasn't that he didn't like it here—the place was magical. A silent lake bordered the property, and it felt as if it belonged exclusively to this parcel of land. But he could see it was huge in size. The neighboring properties would border it too. And on the other side a huge state forest or something equally large loomed.

But even though the place felt magical he still felt uncomfortable. It had been so long since he'd been around people who weren't soldiers. So long since he'd been able to just relax, act like a normal human being.

He looked back to the house again and saw that Lisa was outside now, walking toward him. She was hard not to watch. There was an openness, a kindness about her face that seemed to draw him in. But these days that kind of face was more terrifying to him than armed insurgents. It made him more nervous, more unsure, than any wartime scenario.

"You like it out here?" she asked as she approached him.

He looked back at the water. "It's pretty special."

She moved to stand right next to him. He didn't look at her.

"I've lived in Alaska all my life, and when I saw this place I knew I'd live here forever," she said wistfully.

He envied her that—having a place to call home all your life. He'd moved from town to town into different foster homes before he'd been old enough to escape that life. Having a house, a place, anything that remained the same, was something he'd always wished for.

"You mentioned you wanted to do some fishing?" she prompted.

Alex nodded. He hooked his thumb over his shoulder to point. "I've got my rod, a sleeping bag and some camping equipment in the car. Thought I'd just see where the wind took me for a while."

He could feel her eyes roving over him. It made him feel uncertain.

"But you were planning on staying in Alaska?"

He shrugged. Perhaps.

Lisa turned away and started walking. He didn't want to watch her but he couldn't help it. She had tight jeans on that hugged her legs, ballet flats covering her feet, and a T-shirt that skimmed her curves. He swallowed a lump of…what? It had been so long since he'd felt attracted to a woman that he didn't know what to think.

He ground his teeth. What he had to think of was that she had belonged to someone else—to the very man who had taken a bullet for him. And she was also someone's mommy.

He determinedly averted his gaze.

"Alex, there's something I want to show you."

His head snapped up. Maybe if he'd been better at sticking to the plan he wouldn't be torturing himself like this.

Still, it would be rude not to follow her.

He started to walk. Then stopped when he saw her standing at the foot of a hodge-podge-looking cabin perched behind a cluster of low trees. He hadn't even noticed it before. Although if you weren't looking it wasn't exactly visible for all to see.

Lisa pushed at the door, and he watched as it slowly fell open. She stood back and gestured to him with one hand. "Come have a look."

He obeyed. He had no idea what he was looking for, but he had a scout around with his eyes. The interior was dim. Light filtered in through grubby windowpanes, it smelt a touch musty, and there was an old bed lying forlorn in the corner.

He looked at her for an answer.

She smiled. "If you're looking for a place to bunk down for a while, we'd love to have you."

Alex looked from Lisa, where she stood on the grass outside still, back into the cabin. Stay? Here?

She must have seen the scared rabbit look on his face.

"I mean, just until you figure out where you want to go. A couple of weeks, perhaps?" she offered gently.

He kept staring at her incredulously. He couldn't help it.

"It's not that I wouldn't want you to stay in the house. I just thought you'd prefer some space," she went on.

He shook his head. A slow movement at first that built up to something faster. "Lisa, I…"

"No, don't refuse." She ignored his frantic head-shaking and started to walk back toward the water. It was only meters from the cabin—so close you could practically swing through the trees and land in it.

She swung back around to face him. "I need to fix the cottage up, and it's not like I'm ever going to be able to do it myself. Please. You can stay, fish, help me out, then move on once it's done."

He didn't know what to say. It wasn't that he didn't like the idea of staying here. The place was great. But how could he take up this kind of hospitality knowing that her husband wasn't coming home because he'd chosen to save Alex's life? How could he look at that little girl every day and know that he was the reason she wasn't going to see her daddy ever again?

"I can't stay." His voice was gruff but resolute.

"Alex." She moved closer to him. He saw her hand hover, as though she was about to touch him, and then she crossed her arms. Perhaps she'd already sensed he was damaged goods. "Please. It would mean a lot to me."

Until he braved telling her the truth.

He ignored the familiar trickle of guilt. It had followed him his whole life, was something he was used to living with. But he still recognized it.

"I don't..." He clenched his fists in frustration at not knowing the right thing to say.

She waited patiently.

"You don't want me here," he finally gritted out.

She looked surprised. This time she did reach for him.

He tried to ignore the flicker within him at her touch. There was something too intimate, too close, about seeing her fingers over his forearm. He didn't want to be touched by her.

"I *do* want you here," she insisted. "To be honest, I'd appreciate the company. And fixing this place up was meant to be William's task once he came home."

He fought not to grind his teeth. There was the guilt again. If William hadn't sacrificed his own life for Alex's he'd be here, home, attending to the cabin himself.

"Think on it. If you do decide to stay you'll be helping me out, and you'd have somewhere to fish," she wheedled with a smile.

Her grin was infectious. He didn't know when he'd last wanted to laugh, but she was having some sort of effect on him.

"I don't know," he muttered, but he saw a flicker of something cross her face. She knew he was cracking.

"Just say you'll think about it," she insisted.

He nodded. Just a hint of a nod, but she didn't miss it.

"You think it'll take just two or three weeks to fix this place up?" he asked warily.

She nodded, a gleam of obvious triumph in her eyes.

Alex sighed. It wasn't like he had anywhere else to go. And he owed it to her to help out. "Okay, I'll stay for a while," he said.

"Great!"

He still wasn't completely sure about it, but at least he could do something for her. He had no plans. No direction. He'd just wanted to give her William's things and then spend some time alone. Find himself. Think.

He looked around. The water twinkled at him. The trees seemed to wave. The cabin looked sturdy, albeit rundown.

There were plenty of worse places he could have ended up.

Besides, it was just a few weeks.

"It feels like the right thing, you know, having you here for a while. Makes me feel like part of William is here with you," she said softly.

"Thanks, ma'am. I really appreciate it." He did. Even if he found it hard to show. Foster care did that to you. Stripped you of emotion. Besides guilt and anger, that was. The army hadn't helped much either.

She just smiled.

"I'll make sure to stay out of your way," he added.

Lisa shook her head. "You don't need to stay out of my way. But you might want to stay in the house again tonight, until we've had a bit of a tidy up in here."

He nodded his agreement.

"Come on—I'll show you around," she offered.

Alex fell into step beside her. "You been here a long time?"

Lisa slowed so their steps matched. "We moved here before we were married. It's the kind of place you find and never want to leave."

He liked that. The idea of having a place that you knew would make you happy for life.

"You have a place that you want to settle now that you're a civilian?" she asked.

He shook his head politely, but it was hard to unclamp his jaw to find words.

She glanced at him. Made eye contact briefly. He read her face, knew that she hadn't meant to make him uncomfortable.

"I grew up here. Alaska born and bred," she continued.

Much better. He could listen to her talk all day so long as he could keep his own mouth shut about his past. Some things were better left forgotten.

Like where he was from. Family. And why he had no one in his life besides the army. Army life *was* family life for him. It was virtually all he'd ever known.

Lisa didn't know quite what to feel. Had she pushed Alex too hard? The last few hours had passed pleasantly, but she was worried about forcing him if he wasn't ready.

Maybe she had been a touch insistent. But that was beside the point. He needed a place to stay—somewhere to just be himself and work through the issues he'd brought home with him.

She could do with the company, and Lilly could do with whatever it was that Alex did to her. Her face hadn't lost the shine it had enjoyed all morning. Not a word had been said, but her actions had been more than obvious. The girl was happy and, lately, that was rare.

Alex was a mystery, though. Why did he have nowhere to go? No family? At least none that he wanted to talk about?

She hoped he'd tell her. Eventually. But she only had a few weeks to coax it out of him—unless he decided to stay on longer. But the flighty look in his eyes told her that staying put was not part of his plan.

Alex hacked at the over-hanging branches as if they'd done him some serious harm in the past. He had acquired a good pile already. A body of leaves, branches and debris littered the ground beside him.

It felt good to work up a sweat.

The morning air was coolish, but nice against his hot skin. His stomach was growling for breakfast but he ignored it. Even when it hissed and spat like a cougar.

Yesterday he'd had mixed feelings about staying. Issues about hanging around. But this morning everything seemed different. Maybe it was the good night's sleep—his first in a while—or maybe the fresh air was doing something to him, but he just felt different. And it was good to be doing something positive.

It was still unnerving. Being around William's family. Staying in another man's house. But William was gone now, and Alex had made him a promise. He might have fulfilled that promise, passing William's widow the items and telling her the words, but what kind of man would he be to come all this way and not help a woman in need? He owed it to the man. Owed him his life, in fact.

Even without this drawing them together, making him feel closer to William even though he had passed away, he and William had shared a bond. They had been in the same small unit more than once, and being posted to the places they had been sent meant they'd shared a kind of trust that was hard to explain. It was what made being here even harder—because he knew how much William had cherished what he'd left behind to serve his country.

Alex might have lost his family young, but honor and integrity were high on his list of morals. Of values. He knew how different his own life might have turned out if he'd had his family, if he hadn't lost everything as a child. Even the memories he'd clung to all these years didn't make up for what he'd lost. So he knew how important this little family was.

Lisa and Lilly only had each other now, and if she wanted the cabin fixed up he was happy to be of assistance. It was *his duty* to be there for them, to serve them.

Part of him hoped that staying, doing what he could, would help him put some demons to rest. But even if it only gave him peace of mind for a short time it would be a welcome reprieve from the guilt he had lived with of late.

He looked up at the cabin. It was shabby, there was no denying it, but it was habitable. Plus the view was incredible. Deciding to stay here might be the best decision he'd made in a long time.

He was officially discharged from the army, and he had no idea what he wanted to do. There was enough money in his savings account to keep him going for a while—a very long while—and he didn't want to start anything until his head was clear.

He just wanted to work with his hands. Fish. Chill.

And preferably not get too attached to his host family if he could help it.

"Morning."

He looked up. Lisa was watching him. She was dressed, but she still had that early morning glow. Her hair was wet, hanging down over her shoulders, leaving a damp mark on her T-shirt that he could see from here. She was nursing a cup of something hot.

"Morning," he replied. He reached for his own T-shirt, tucked into the back of his jeans, and tugged it on.

"You've been busy," she remarked.

He stepped back and looked at the mess he'd made. "Too much?"

She laughed. "I don't think any amount of work in or around that cabin could be called too much."

He wasn't used to casual chat with a woman anymore, but he was starting to warm to her. She was so easy, so relaxed. As if she expected nothing from him. Yet he knew she'd expect more. An answer. An explanation.

He swallowed the worry.

"You ready for some breakfast?"

His stomach doubled over in response. "I didn't want to go poking around in the cupboards."

She motioned with her hand for him to follow. "You're welcome to anything we've got here. Make yourself at home."

If only she knew how promising that sounded to him. Only he didn't really know how to make himself at home anywhere. Except in an army camp, perhaps.

"I hope you're hungry." She threw a glance over his shoulder.

"Yes, ma'am."

Lisa stopped and gave him one of those heart-warming smiles. "Good—because I've got eggs, bacon and sausages in the pan for you."

He'd never thought breakfast could sound so good.

"Oh, and Alex?"

He walked two beats faster to catch up with her step.

"Please don't call me ma'am again. It makes me feel like an old lady."

He sucked a lungful of air and fell back a pace or two behind her. And wished he hadn't. He had to fight not to look at the sway of her hips.

The term *old lady* hadn't crossed his mind when he'd looked at her. Ever.

Lisa patted the bacon down with a paper towel to absorb the grease and then placed it on a large plate. She saved a rasher for herself, and slipped the spatula beneath the eggs to turn them. She hoped he liked them easy-over.

"Do I take all your work out there this morning as notice that you're definitely staying?" She didn't look over her shoulder, just continued getting breakfast ready. She thought he'd feel less pressured without her watching his face.

"Ah…I guess you could say that," he answered warily.

She pursed her lips to stop from smiling. "Excellent." She spun around and just about tossed the plate and its entire contents over Alex. "Oh!"

He moved quickly, grabbing the plate and steadying her with the other hand.

"Sorry. I was just…"

She felt a sense of cool as his hand left her upper arm.

"…going to help you with the plate," he finished.

Lisa felt bad that his tanned cheeks had a hue of crimson adorning them.

"Aren't you having any?" he asked in concern, looking at how much she'd given him.

That made her smile. She couldn't cook breakfast and not partake. "Just a small version for me."

She sat down at the table with him, her own plate modestly loaded. His hands hovered over the utensils.

"Please start," she told him, wanting to put him at ease. "Eat while it's hot."

He did.

She watched as he firmly yet politely pierced meat and cut at his toast, practically inhaling the breakfast. She wondered if she'd served him enough.

"I've got work to do today, so I'm not going to be any help to you out there," she said.

Alex placed his knife and fork on the edge of the plate and reached for his coffee. She forced herself not to watch his every move. Strong fingers curled around the cup and he wiped at the corner of his mouth with the other hand.

"Where do you work?" he asked.

She was pleased he'd asked. Maybe food *was* the way to communicate with a man after all.

"I work from home," she explained, rising to collect the toast she'd left cooling in a rack on the counter. She brought it back to the table. "As I mentioned before, I write cookbooks, so I'm usually trying out new recipes, baking things."

He swallowed another mouthful of coffee. "Right."

"And today I'm under pressure, because my editor wants recipes emailed to her by the end of next week."

He looked thoughtful. She opened a jar of homemade jam and nudged it toward him. Alex dipped a knife in and spread some on a piece of toast.

"Do you have to take Lilly to school soon?"

She shook her head. "Spring break." She sighed. "But she hasn't gone back to school since William died, so I've had to start home-schooling her."

Alex looked like he was calculating how long that was.

"I do my best, but I need to get her back there." She sighed.

"Have you tried therapy?" he asked.

She blew out a deep breath. "Yup."

She couldn't tell if he approved or not. For some reason his opinion mattered to her.

"I'd better get back out there," he said.

She rose as he did, and collected the plates.

"Thanks for breakfast," he added.

He looked awkward but she ignored it. "No problem. I owe you for taking on the jungle out there."

The look he gave her made her think otherwise. That he thought *he* owed *her*. The way his eyes flickered, briefly catching hers, almost questioning.

"You need a hand with those?" he offered.

Lisa turned back to him. To those sad eyes trained her way. "I'm fine here. I'll have lunch ready for later, but help yourself to anything you need. The door's open."

She watched as Alex walked out. His shoulders were so broad, yet they looked like they were frowning. He looked so strong, yet sad—tough, yet soft. As if he could crush an enemy with his bare hands, yet provide comfort to one of his own all in the same breath.

She wished there was more she could do for him. But something told her that whatever she was doing was enough for now.

Lisa looked out the window as he appeared nearby. He

reached for the ax and dragged it upward in the air before slicing through a tree stump. She felt naughty watching him. Indulging in seeing his muscles flex and work, seeing the tension on his face drain away as he started to gather momentum.

She would be forever grateful that he'd come all this way to give her William's things. It had given her some sort of closure. Made his passing more final, somehow.

The tags Alex had given her had been William's older ones— the more current ones had come home with his body—but she had taken comfort in wearing them.

This morning she had tucked them in her jewellery box, along with the folded letters and the photo of Lilly.

She had made a decision too.

To stop grieving. To be brave and take a big step forward.

William was gone. It had taken her a long while to admit that.

He'd been a great husband and an even better father. But he'd also been a soldier. And that meant she'd always known that this day, being alone, could come, and she had to face it.

The reality of being a soldier's wife was that you had to risk losing him. That you couldn't hold him back.

Well, she'd loved William with all her heart, but she'd also accepted that his being a soldier, facing live combat, could mean he could be taken from her.

And he had.

This was the first day of her new life as a woman dealing with life, accepting what had happened to her, and being the best mother she could be. Not a widow. The word was so full of grief, so depressing, and if she stopped thinking of herself that way it might make it easier to move forward.

She had loved her husband. In her heart she knew no one could ever attempt or threaten to replace William. He had been too special, too important to her.

But she did want to keep a smile on her face and try to be happy. If Alex's company helped her do that, then she wasn't going to feel bad about it.

CHAPTER FOUR

THERE was something nice about having a man in the house again. Although Alex wasn't technically *in* the house, having him in the cabin was equally as good.

She'd never felt nervous, exactly—not out here—but there had always been a certain element of unease that she'd never been able to shake. A longing to have a man at home every night. Someone to protect the fort. Someone in the window if you came home after dark.

It was stupid, but it was true. She was a woman and she liked to feel protected and nurtured.

The phone rang. She saw the caller identification as it flashed across the little screen.

Great.

Lisa had been avoiding her sister since Alex had arrived, but Anna wasn't someone who took to being avoided very well. Her mother? Well, she wasn't so bad, but her sister could be downright painful sometimes.

"Hey, Anna." She put on her best sing-song voice as she answered the phone. If Lisa didn't talk to her now, Anna would be likely to turn up here before dark to check on her.

"Hello, stranger."

Lisa could tell her sister was worried. She had that slightly high-pitched note to her voice. "Sorry, hon, I've just been flat out trying to get these recipes in order."

"You still need a life, though, right?" Anna said.

Lisa glanced out the window and spied Alex working on a cabin window. He was trying to force it open. Did having him here constitute having a life?

"Hmm, I know. I just want this book to be good."

"They're always good," her sister replied instantly.

The vote of confidence helped.

"How about you and some of the girls come by on Saturday afternoon for a tasting?" Lisa suggested.

"Love to. Want me to organize it?"

"Sounds good," Lisa agreed.

"Just the usual gang?" Anna asked.

Five women were plenty, Lisa thought. "Yup—and Mom."

She heard Anna flicking through what she presumed was her calendar. That girl knew what everyone was up to!

"Nope. Mom has that charity fundraiser meeting going on. I'll tell her you asked, though," Anna said.

Lisa tucked the phone beneath her ear and rinsed her hands in the sink. Her eyes were still firmly locked on Alex.

"You sure you're okay?"

Lisa nodded.

"I can't hear you if you're nodding," her sister said dryly.

Damn it! It was like Anna had secret cameras installed in the house!

"I'm fine. I just need to get all this sorted," Lisa told her.

"Need me to come by?" Anna asked.

"No!" she yelled. "I mean, no. I'm fine." The silence on the other end told her she hadn't convinced her sister. "Come by with the girls on Saturday afternoon. I just need some time and we'll catch up then, okay?"

As Lisa said her goodbyes and hung up the phone she felt guilty. She usually shared everything with her sister. Everything. And yet she had a very big something hanging around out back, staying with her for the next few weeks, and she had omitted even to mention it.

Lilly was marching back and forth outside, Boston at her

heels. She had a huge stick in her hand—one that Alex had no doubt cut down before she'd claimed it.

Lisa went about fiddling with quantities and ingredients, dragging her eyes from the window.

She couldn't deny that she liked what she saw. But then what woman wouldn't?

Alex walked inside with Lilly on his hip. He'd thought the dog was going to attack when he'd first picked her up, but after a few gentle words and a futile attempt to stop the kid crying he had hoisted her up and into the house.

But his feet had stopped before they'd found her mom.

Lilly's cries had become diluted to gentle hiccups. It was awkward, holding her so close, but he'd had little choice. It had been a very long time since he'd held another human being like that.

Lisa was swaying in time to the beat of the music playing loudly in the kitchen. Her hair was caught back off her face with a spotted kerchief, and she had a splodge or two of flour on her cheek. The pink apron added to his discomfort. It had pulled her top down with it, and she was displaying more cleavage than he guessed she would usually show.

And she still hadn't noticed them above the hum of the music.

"Huh-hmm." He cleared his throat. Then again—louder.

She looked up, lips moving to the lyrics. Her mouth stopped, wide open, before she clamped it shut.

Lilly burst into much louder tears as soon as her mother noticed her, and all Alex could do was hold her out at a peculiar angle until Lisa swept her into her own arms.

"Baby, what happened?"

The lips that had been singing and smiling only moments earlier fell in a series of tiny kisses to her daughter's head. Lisa nursed her as she moved to turn off the speaker that was belting out the tunes.

"Shh, now. It's all right—you just got a fright," Lisa crooned.

She hugged her daughter tight. Alex couldn't take his eyes off them. It tugged something inside him, pushed at something that he hadn't felt in a long while.

"How about Alex tells me what happened while you catch your breath?" she murmured.

He cringed. Taking care of kids wasn't his thing. This one might have taken a shine to him, but he had no experience. No idea at all. "I'm sorry, she just...ah...she fell from a tree. I should have been watching her. I..."

Lisa drew her eyebrows together and waved at him with her free hand. "She's a child, Alex. And she's *my* child. If anyone should feel bad for not watching her it's me."

A touch of weight left his shoulders. But not all of it.

"I was..."

"Enough." She put Lilly down and crouched beside her. "If you wrap children in cotton wool they can't have any fun. Tumbles and bruises are all part of being a child."

He swallowed. Hard. She was inspecting Lilly, checking her, but she wasn't angry.

"You're fine, honey. How about you go play in your room for a while? Take it easy, okay?"

Lilly was still doing the odd snuffle, but Lisa simply gave her a pat on the head and blew her a kiss.

"I'm sorry," he muttered.

"Alex! For the last time, it was *not* your fault. Do I look angry?" she asked.

He ran his eyes over her face. He had seen her look worried before, concerned, but, no, not angry.

She obviously wasn't like most moms.

"You're just in time to try a few things," she said, changing the subject.

That sounded scary. He followed her, then sat down at the counter. Same spot he'd ended up when he'd arrived.

"I want your opinion on this slice. And this pastry."

That didn't sound too hard, he thought.

She straightened her apron and wiped at her cheek. He was almost disappointed when the smudge disappeared.

"What's your book called?" he asked curiously.

She turned around, turning her wide smile on him. "I'm thinking *Lisa's Treats*, but my editor will probably have other ideas."

Huh? "Doesn't that bother you?"

She fiddled with a tray, then scooped a tiny pastry something onto her fingers.

"What?"

"Not being able to choose the title yourself?" he explained.

She raised an eyebrow before lifting the pastry to his mouth. He opened it. How could he not? She was holding something that smelt delicious in front of it.

"They know how to sell books. I just know how to write what's inside. Good?"

He swallowed. *Very good.* "Good," he agreed.

"Just good?" she probed.

That made him nervous. Hadn't she just asked for good? "Great?" he tried.

"Hmm, I'd prefer excellent." She whisked away, and then twirled back to him. "Try this."

Once again she thrust something into his mouth.

Oh. Yes. "Incredible."

"Good." She had a triumphant look on her face.

He was still confused, but he tried to stay focused on the food. If he didn't look at the food he'd have to look at her. And the niggle in his chest was telling him that could be dangerous. Very dangerous.

"And this?"

This time when she twirled around she had a spoon covered in a gooey mixture. It looked decadent. Delicious. Just like her.

"Last up—my new chocolate icing."

She leaned across the counter toward him. Too close. He

fought the urge to lean back, to literally fall off the stool to get away from her. Lisa's eyes danced over his. The connection between them scared him rigid.

He sucked air through his nostrils and tried to stop his hands from becoming clammy.

Lisa held the spoon in the air, waiting for him to taste from it. He gathered courage and obeyed, his face ending up way too close to hers.

"Good?"

He could almost feel her breath on his skin. Or was he imagining it? He raised his eyes an inch. She didn't pull away. There was a beat where he wondered if she ever would.

"Excellent." He was learning how to play this game. Praise at least one word higher than what she'd asked for.

"Okay—that's me done for the day, then," she announced briskly.

She walked away from him fast. Like she'd been burnt. The flush over his own skin was making him feel the same. He glanced around the kitchen. At the trays littered across the bench, the dishes piled in the sink and the ingredients scattered. Maybe it would be polite to help, but he needed to get out of here. Put some distance between them.

Yet still he lingered. Good manners overrode emotion.

"Want a hand with all this?" he asked tentatively.

She gave him a cheeky grin. "Want a hand outside?"

Alex shrugged his acquiescence. Inside, his lungs screamed.

"Great, then I'll leave this till later," she told him happily.

Two hours later Alex was still working outside while she tinkered inside the cabin. She flicked a duster around all the surfaces, before giving the bed a good thump and making it with the linen she'd brought out.

She liked having him here. Every hour that passed she couldn't help but think she'd done the right thing asking him to stay. It wasn't just the effect he had on Lilly, he affected her too.

All went quiet outside, and he appeared in the doorway. His body filled the entire frame.

"How you getting on out there?" she asked. She could see a line of sweat starting to make a trickle across his forehead. It made her gulp. He was…well, very manly. And it was doing something to her, if the caged bird beating its wings with fury inside her stomach was any sort of gauge.

"Getting there."

She used her head to indicate where the water was. He followed.

"Thinking it will take longer to get this place habitable?" she asked.

He shook his head.

If she'd just spent years at war, and years before that in army bunkers, she'd probably think the cabin wasn't half bad either. Lisa fiddled with the duster and then stopped. She pinned her eyes on him. "Alex, I was thinking—did you actually see…you know…how William died?"

His shoulders hunched. He stopped guzzling water like he'd just emerged from the desert and stayed still. Deathly still.

So he *did* know.

It didn't matter if he didn't want to tell her. She already knew William had died from multiple bullet wounds. She'd just always wondered *how. Why?* What had actually happened over there? Who had fired? For what reason?

He dropped to an armchair in the corner. Dust thumped out of it but he seemed oblivious to it. Lisa knew she'd been wrong in asking so soon, but she couldn't take it back. Not yet. Not now.

The question hung between them.

"We were…" He took a long pause before continuing. "I mean, we came under fire."

She sat down too. On the bed. Despite just having made it.

"They think there was one, maybe two guys waiting for us. Snipers."

She could see the torment on his face. The emotion of pulling memories to the surface again. But she wanted to know.

"I'm sorry. I can't talk about it." Alex jumped to his feet and walked out the door. Fast.

Lisa sighed. She should never have pushed him. It was too early to be asking him things like that. Things that didn't really matter anymore. Not when nothing could be done about it.

"Alex, wait." She rushed out after him.

Emotion seeped from him. She could see it. Feel it. Smell it. He practically radiated hurt and confusion as she walked slowly up behind him. He had one hand braced against a tree. The other hung at his side. She stopped inches away from him, her body close to his. She didn't touch him.

"I'm sorry, Alex. I had no right to ask you that."

In a way she was lying. She *did* have the right to know. But not yet. Not until he was ready to tell.

She stood there for a moment. Watching him. Waiting. "We need some ground rules. If you want to talk about what happened, you can—anytime." She paused. "But I won't ask you about it again."

She sensed relief from him. He swiveled—just slightly, but their eyes met. She understood. She still struggled with telling people that William was gone sometimes. Felt all alone and lost.

"When you're ready to talk, tell me," she reiterated.

He just stared at her. His eyes acknowledged her words with a faint flicker.

"Sound okay to you?" she pressed.

"Yeah." His voice lacked punch.

Lisa turned and went back into the cabin. He needed some tender loving care. There was obviously no one to give it to him. But she wasn't going to ask him about that either.

This had to be a safe place for him. A place where there was no pressure and where nobody asked him questions they had no right to ask. At least not yet. Not before he trusted her. Not until she had made him feel comfortable enough to talk. Not until he'd had time.

And she wanted him to hang around, so the last thing she was going to do was push him away. He made her feel close to William, somehow. Comforted her.

Alex lay on the bed. It was almost too short for him, but if he kept his legs slightly bent he fit fine. Besides, it wasn't the bed that was stopping him from falling asleep.

It was Lisa.

Every time he closed his eyes he saw her. Sometimes Lilly was there as well. But he saw Lisa every time.

When they were open he saw her too.

It was a no-win situation.

Today had been tough. The hard labor had done him good, fired him up and taken the edge off his turbulent emotions. But being in such close proximity to a woman he found so darn attractive had put even more strain on him.

He was guilty. Guilty as a man who'd just committed a crime. Guilty as a bird who'd just stolen a piece of bread. And he hated it.

When he'd agreed to come here, to visit William's widow, he'd formed a picture in his mind of what it would be like. She would be plain, pleasant, standing in the doorway with a child beside her and one hand on an extended pregnant stomach. She would fall to her knees crying as he said the words he'd rehearsed. He'd pass her the things, put one hand on her shoulder as comfort, then turn and walk away.

Turning back had never been part of the plan. Neither had getting caught up in the emotion of her pain.

But then he'd also banked on the guilt falling away once he'd fulfilled his promise. Rather than wishing the woman before him was his own wife and that he'd just arrived back home. Or that he could just die, then and there, and give her her husband back.

He felt the excruciating guilt again now, like a knife through his chest. Saw everything flash beneath his eyelids as if it was happening all over again.

He turned as William called his name. So fast, so quick. He looked up, tripped as William launched himself at him and threw him to the ground.

A round of bullets echoed just before they hit the ground, then more. Punching through the air. Then the wet, warm splatter of blood hit him in the face.

He opened his eyes and found William staring at him, gasping.

The sniper was gone. Silence thrummed through the air like it was alive.

He moved William off him, gently. Placed him on the ground, on his back, propping his head up and listening hard to his rasping words. William ordered him to take the photo in his pocket, scrawled the name and address of his wife, then whispered words for her. He told him where to find the letters he had waiting for her at camp. To give them to her. To find her. Then he took his last breath.

Alex sat up, exhausted from his own thoughts. He dropped his head into his hands. How had this situation become so complicated? He could get up right now. Get up and leave. Start driving and never look back. But could he? Really? Could he just turn his back on Lisa and Lilly now?

He knew the answer to that. He'd only known them such a short time, and yet he felt something between them. He and Lilly understood one another, even though they didn't talk. He didn't get what to do around kids a lot of the time, but he knew about loss, about heartache. Especially about losing a parent. Or in his case both.

A shudder ran down his back—the same shudder that always came when he thought about his parents. About the other time he'd been splattered with blood that wasn't his own.

It was as if he'd cheated death twice. As if the grim reaper had come for him and somehow he'd managed to avoid him.

Twice. His parents had been taken, his friend had been taken, and yet he was still standing. Why?

The image in his mind turned back to Lisa, and the feeling of sadness that had just ruptured inside him was replaced by harrowing guilt once again.

If he'd ever fantasized about the kind of woman he could settle down with, he knew the picture would have looked a lot like her. Beautiful, so beautiful, and yet so much more. She had a way about her—a way of looking at a person or situation with complete understanding. He'd been so impressed with how she'd handled Lilly's fall today. Careful, methodical in checking her, yet not allowing the child to make a fuss.

And she was dealing with her daughter's inability to communicate with others well too. She must feel worried, but she stayed calm. Treated Lilly as if nothing had changed.

Alex knew first-hand what being in Lilly's shoes was like, and he wished he had the courage to tell Lisa how well she was doing. That she was doing the right thing.

Lisa. Her name consumed his mind.

He was attracted to her. More than attracted to her, he realized. But he wouldn't act on it.

Couldn't.

If it wasn't for him her husband would be coming home after his term serving overseas. If it wasn't for him her daughter wouldn't be traumatized. Grieving.

But he wasn't going to run out on them.

He lay back down and squeezed his eyes shut.

If he wasn't entertaining such intimate thoughts about another man's wife, maybe sleep would have found him by now.

CHAPTER FIVE

LISA resisted the urge to swipe her finger through the lemon icing as she arranged the cakes on a tray. It was stupid, but she was nervous.

Before she ever sent a book away to her editor she always hosted an afternoon get-together, so it wasn't like she had first-time jitters. Besides, they were her friends coming over—not a bunch of strangers. But there was something about living in a small town that jangled your nerves when it came to gossip.

When you knew it was you who was about to become the center of it.

She shrugged off the worry and rolled her shoulders. The knot at the base of her neck didn't disappear, but she felt a touch more relaxed.

Her kitchen looked ready for some sort of fairy birthday party. Pink macaroons, swirls of lemon zest atop white icing, and just about everything chocolate a girl could want. She hoped it was enough to distract her sister from the man living in her cabin.

She reached for a mini-cake and took a huge bite. The sugar rush made her feel mildly better, but she still felt as if she was doing something illicit.

A tap at the door made Lisa swallow fast, lick the icing from her teeth and throw the rest of the cake in the trash. She heard footsteps echo down the hall.

It was her sister. The other girls would wait to be let in.

"Hi!"

Yes, definitely Anna.

I am a grown woman, she chanted silently. I have nothing to be ashamed of. I still love my husband. Alex is only staying because he has nowhere else to go. Because he can help me out.

"There you are." Anna passed her a bunch of flowers and kissed her cheek.

"You're early," Lisa said.

"Hardly." Anna ran her eyes over the food. "Looks delicious."

Lisa walked the flowers into the kitchen and dropped them on the counter. She reached for a vase and filled it with water.

"So, little sis, what's been happening?"

"Nothing." Lisa took a breath and turned the water off. "I mean...you know—just working on recipes, baking up a storm, that kind of thing."

"Huh."

She didn't like that noise. It was the noise Anna always made when she knew something was up. When she didn't believe her but was happy to let it lie. Temporarily.

Lisa glanced at the cabin and prayed that Alex wouldn't emerge. Or be anywhere within sight of the kitchen or lounge for the next hour.

"Lisa, I..."

A rumble of heels on timber followed by a knock saved her.

"Anna, be a gem and get the door, would you?"

Her sister paused, gave her a look, and walked out.

Lisa leaned against the counter and tried to calm down. This was awful. She'd never been good at secrets—especially not ones like this.

She forced herself to fiddle with the flowers, set the vase on the center island and took a final look at the goodies.

This was going to be a long, long afternoon.

* * *

"Lisa, this is amazing!"

"Mmm."

She grinned as her friends licked at their lips and reached for more.

"You know you *are* allowed to say when you don't like something," she said.

"Honey, you're the best. You know you are, or people would stop buying your books," Anna defended her loyally.

She leaned into her sister and laughed. "You're family—you have to say that."

Lisa looked up as she heard a noise. Please, don't let it be Alex. Surely he wouldn't have just changed his mind and walked in? She'd told him the girls were coming over, and his joining them had seemed to be less likely than him pouring out his heart to her.

"Mom!" She jumped to her feet. What was her mother doing here?

"Hello, darling."

Lisa looked at Anna. Her sister just shrugged.

"I thought you had a meeting today?" Lisa said.

"Turns out I managed to sneak away," her mother replied with a smile.

She smelled a rat. They had a group attack planned. She could feel it.

"Where's my granddaughter?"

Lisa watched as her mother folded her sweater over a chair and placed her handbag on top of it.

"Yes, where *is* Lilly?" Now Anna was looking around.

"She's just out playing with Boston. Looking for bugs, climbing trees." Lisa took a deep lungful of air and determined to slow her voice.

Nothing got past those two, though. While her friends kept nattering and sipping coffee, her mother and sister were watching her as if she was up to something.

"Oh—my—word."

Lisa's head swiveled to lock eyes on her friend Sandra. A crawl of dread trickled sideways through her stomach.

"Who is *that*?"

Lisa squeezed her eyes shut for a moment, then looked out the window. Every woman in the room had her eyes trained on the exact same spot.

At least he had his shirt on. The other day, when she'd caught a glimpse of his bare chest, she'd realized the sight was enough to send any woman crazy.

Alex was standing next to Lilly. The pair of them were side by side as he demonstrated how to throw the fishing line into the water. Lilly had her tongue caught between her teeth, was trying hard to mimic him, but the rod was almost as big as she was.

Lisa saw him as her friends would. Big, strong man, with shoulders almost as wide as Lilly was long. Muscled forearms tensing as he cast the line back and forward.

He bent over to correct Lilly's grip and almost ended up wearing a piece of bait in his eye. She started laughing. It took a moment, but Alex started too. They both stood there, this giant and his fairy, giggling.

Lisa had never seen anything like it.

Had Lilly even laughed like that once since she'd been silent? It looked so natural. Seeing Lilly respond like that to Alex was special. Very special.

"Huh-hmm."

Lisa realized where she was again.

"Yes, Lisa. Who *is* that man cavorting with your daughter?" her sister asked pointedly.

She decided not to turn to face Anna. "I wouldn't say he was *cavorting*, exactly."

She grimaced and waited for it. Sandra spoke before her sister had a chance to reply.

"I don't care what he's doing, but I wish he was doing something to me!"

That set the whole room off laughing.

"Enough, ladies, enough." Lisa pulled herself away from the window and faced the room. "He's just an old friend of William's come to visit. The last thing he needs is us ogling him. Besides, you're all married."

The women kept their eyes on the view.

"I'll get some more coffee," she muttered.

"And I'll help," snapped Anna.

Her sister grabbed her elbow and marched her to the kitchen.

She guessed that talking about the handsome man outside the window was non-negotiable.

Lisa chanced a glance at her sister's face.

Definitely non-negotiable.

But she didn't have to tell them that he was living in the cabin.

No way.

Lisa felt as if she'd been a very naughty girl. Hell, she was thirty years old, not thirteen, and yet somehow she was still cast as the little sister. Was that something she was stuck with for life?

"Start talking," Anna ordered.

She straightened her shoulders, evaded her sister's stare and filled the jug with water. "There's nothing to tell. I don't know why you're making such a fuss."

"Such a fuss!" Anna threw her hands in the air. "Lisa, you've been avoiding me for days, then I find out you've got a man here. Are you seeing him?"

She glared. "Don't you *dare* ask me that!" Lisa growled the words at her. How could Anna accuse her of seeing another man? Every beat of her heart reminded her she still loved William. She might be attracted to Alex, but she was not doing anything inappropriate.

Anna just shrugged.

Her mother walked in. "I've heard enough, girls."

They both kept their mouths shut. They knew better than to argue with her when she spoke in that tone of voice.

"Let Lisa explain."

Huh. So she wasn't exactly off the hook.

Lisa pulled out a seat at the counter and sat down. Her neck was aching, shoulders tense, and she was exhausted. Like she'd run a marathon twice over. "His name is Alex. He served with William and he needed a place to stay."

"Stay!" Her sister nearly exploded.

A sharp look from their mother silenced her.

"Yes, stay," Lisa repeated. "And don't go jumping to any conclusions."

Anna kept her mouth shut for once.

"It's nice he felt he could come here," their mother remarked calmly.

Lisa smiled at her mother. "He's got some…well, some traumas to work through, and it just seemed like the right thing to do."

Anna still didn't look impressed, but Lisa ignored her.

"I see Lilly's taken a shine to him?"

Lisa's face was hot and flushed. The last thing she wanted was for her mother to be hurt. Seeing her granddaughter laughing with a stranger, even if she wasn't saying any actual words to him, was tough. She saw plenty of her grandmother, had done all her life, but she'd been closed off to everyone but Lisa herself up until now.

Except for this stranger. Except for Alex.

"Come on—let's get the coffee out to everyone. They're probably still drooling out the window," Lisa said.

"You still should have told us."

They both turned to look at Anna.

"I mean, how long have you even *known* this guy?"

Lisa put a hand on her mother's arm and gave her sister a narrow smile. "He's not a psychopath, if that's what you're worried about." She put on her bravest face. "And I wasn't trying to hide him. I wouldn't have had you here today if I was worried about you seeing him."

"We might need iced drinks!" A shout from the living room made them all turn. "It's getting hot in here!"

Lisa prayed that Alex hadn't taken off his shirt. Heavens, she'd have the girls here all evening if he had!

Lisa shut the door with a satisfied bang and leaned against it. The timber felt cool against her back. She'd been naïve to think her friends seeing Alex would go down without some interest, but she had been surprised by her sister's reaction.

The fact that her sister was still in her kitchen wasn't helping either.

Her mother she wasn't so worried about. But Anna?

She had as good as idolized William. The two of them had always gotten on well, right from the beginning when Lisa and he had first started dating. Once they were both married they had double-dated, hung out together whenever William was home on leave.

Anna and her husband were Lilly's godparents. They were all best friends. But it didn't mean Anna had a right to judge her.

She was judging herself enough, without needing to worry about others doing it too. Every time she felt her eyes drawn to Alex. Every time she felt a dusting of attraction. It made her feel guilty. Unfaithful.

Where William had been chatty and bright, like an energetic ball of sunshine, Alex was brooding. Lost in thought. Closed.

But she couldn't help the way she felt. The way she wanted to help him. Nurture him. Be the one to bring him slowly from his shell. It didn't mean she wanted to move on. At least she didn't think so. Confusion danced a pattern through her mind.

"Almost done, dear."

She smiled as her mother crossed the hall. "Thanks."

"Are you feeling okay?"

Lisa nodded. Her mother walked a few steps closer. "You should have told us, Lisa, just for your own safety. But this is your home, and it's your life. William's been gone now for months."

"I'm not *seeing* Alex, Mom." She felt like she was going to cry. Felt unfaithful to her darling husband just having to defend herself.

"Maybe not. But it doesn't mean you shouldn't if you want to."

Lisa swallowed away her emotion and linked arms with her mother. She dropped her head on her shoulder as they walked. Why did it have to be so hard?

"Can you tell Anna that?"

"Does that mean you *are* dating him?" her mother asked.

She flicked her mother on the arm and they both laughed.

No, but it didn't mean she hadn't thought about it. No matter how much her stomach crawled with guilt and worry, she couldn't deny thinking about Alex like that.

"So, do we get to meet this man?" Anna asked waspishly.

Lisa tried her hardest not to roll her eyes. "His name is Alex." She put up a hand before Anna had a chance to speak again. "And, yes, you can meet him right now."

Her mother smiled. Encouragingly.

"I'm just going to pour them each a glass of homemade lemonade and…"

"I'll get some cake," her mother finished.

Lisa filled the tray.

"Come on, then," she said, beckoning with her head. "And go easy on him."

It wasn't that she was worried about how he'd react to them. She'd told him plenty about her family. But he didn't like being asked about his past. His family. Or about war zones. She had picked up on that pretty fast, and she had no intention of pushing him unless he was mentally ready for it.

"Do you think it's okay to leave Lilly with him?"

Lisa ignored Anna's question. Was it okay? The kid hadn't spoken or shown interest in anyone except her and Boston for months, and yet she had taken to this guy like a bear to honey.

And he was hardly likely to hurt her. The man was more frightened of Lilly than she could ever be of him!

Plus, Alex just gave off the right vibes. Sad? Yes. Emotional wreck? Check. But dangerous? Even if *she* had judged his character wrong William wouldn't have. Not after serving with him. If he trusted him enough to send him here, knowing that she'd be alone, then that was all that mattered.

She heard Lilly laughing. If she'd been alone she would have stopped to listen. Wondered at what Alex had said, or done, that she found so funny.

"Lilly! Boston!" Lisa called out to alert them. She didn't want it to seem like she was sneaking up on them. "Anybody hungry?"

Boston appeared first, leaping from the trees and landing on the path in front of them. He sported his usual big smile, tail wagging ferociously.

"Hey, Boston."

Boston was sprinkled with water and his big feet were covered in mud.

A shadow caught Lisa's attention. It was like an umbrella had been whisked across the path. She felt rather than heard Anna go silent. Lisa looked up. And locked eyes with her guest.

"Hey, Alex."

He smiled. Less reserved than the smile he'd given her the day he arrived, but still cautious.

"I wanted to introduce you to some of my family," she told him.

He looked wary. She didn't blame him. She couldn't see the look on her sister's face but she could guess at it. As if he was the enemy. As if somehow this man was to blame for William not coming home.

Lilly suddenly burst from the trees.

"Bost..."

The name died in her mouth as she saw the others.

Lisa gave her a big smile, put down the tray and opened her arms. Lilly didn't hesitate before running to her mother.

"Say hello to Grandma and Anna."

Lilly gave them a wave and a big grin, before turning her eyes back to Alex. If she were older, Lisa would have thought she had a crush on the man.

"Alex, this is my mother, Marj, and my sister Anna." She gestured with her free hand.

"It's lovely to meet you, Alex." Her mother came forward and reached for his hand.

Alex moved slowly. Lisa found herself holding her breath.

"Marj," he said, like he was trying her name out. "I've heard a lot about you."

Lisa practically felt the silent words of her sister hovering in the air. *Wish we'd heard a lot about you.*

"And, Anna," he said, before she could say anything first. "Nice to meet you too." He held out his hand to her.

Anna clasped it. Lisa tried to ignore the tightness of her sister's smile. The way her eyes seemed to question him.

"What brings you to Brownswood?" her sister asked.

Alex looked uncomfortable. There was no way Lisa was going to let him feel bad about being here. Not when he had obviously faced a big battle just turning up here to meet her. She interrupted. "Alex was kind enough to bring some of William's things to me," she explained. Lisa started to walk, giving Alex the opportunity of some breathing space. "He was with William…ah…before his passing."

She glared back at her sister. The news had done little to change the look on her face, but she could see her mother softening.

"That was very kind of you, Alex," Marj said.

He shrugged his shoulders. Lilly squirmed and wriggled in Lisa's arms to get down. She bent and released her.

Boston took up the game and raced after Lilly as she ran, blonde hair streaming out behind her.

Lisa stifled a gasp as she watched. Lilly had caught Alex's hand, just lightly, as she moved past him. Just a touch, just a glimpse of contact, but contact nonetheless.

He didn't react. Well, hardly. But she didn't miss the slight upturn of his fingers. He had made contact back. And she guessed her sister hadn't missed the closeness between man and child either.

"Alex, are you okay taking the tray?" Lisa asked.

He turned around. Embarrassment fell upon his face like a shadow over water. Only he had nothing to be embarrassed about. Lilly was reaching out to him. There was nothing wrong with that.

"Sorry, I…"

"Don't be sorry. I just thought you could take this to the lake while I see these guys off."

He nodded.

"Come on, ladies," Lisa urged.

Her mother didn't hesitate, but Anna gave her another pointed look before saying, "It was lovely to meet you, Alex. Hopefully we'll see you again soon."

They started to walk back to the house. Alex had obviously been a touch uncomfortable, but the meet hadn't gone down too badly.

"He's awfully quiet," said Anna.

Lisa didn't need a thesaurus to figure out the meaning there. Not like William, her sister meant. William who'd worn his heart on his sleeve and been able to natter with the best of women.

"He's just come back from war—isn't that right, Lisa?" Marj said gently.

She nodded at her mother.

"You'd best remember that, Anna, and give the man a break," Marj said.

Lisa sighed. Sometimes having your mom around was the best medicine. It didn't matter what her opinion, or her own view, she was always supporter number one.

"You don't need to see us out, dear." Her mother patted her on the shoulder as they reached the house. "Go enjoy your afternoon."

* * *

Alex sat beside Lilly. He was still struggling with the whole kid thing. Not that she wasn't great, but he just wasn't used to it. Not to the enthusiasm. Not to the unpredictability. Not to the inquisitiveness. And she managed all that without saying a word.

He watched as she bit into a pink cake. He had no idea what the little bite-size sugar rush things were called, but they tasted good.

He listened to footfalls as Lisa approached. He didn't turn. He felt like he was slowly becoming desensitized, but there were things he would never shake. The quietness of the lake, or a bang that could signal danger.

"Hey, there," she said casually.

He liked that about Lisa. It was as if she knew what he was going through—understood, almost.

Alex drew one leg up so he could turn to look at her.

"Good…ah…cake." He held up what was left of the pink item.

"Macaroon," she corrected, dropping to sit beside him. "It's a rosewater macaroon."

He couldn't help the grin that stretched his face. "Rosewater? What happened to plain old strawberry?"

She laughed and reached for a tiny iced treat herself. "Went out with the nineties."

He guessed she saw the confusion cross his face when she started hiccupping with laughter. "Kidding, kidding!" She put up her hand. "I'm just doing a trial on some different things. There's still plenty of room for good old-fashioned flavors."

Lilly stood up and wriggled between them. She glanced up from under her lashes at Alex before cupping Lisa's ear. Then she dropped her hand, like an afterthought, and sat back down.

"Alex is gonna help me catch a real fish tomorrow," the little girl announced clearly.

"Really?" Lisa asked, determinedly nonchalant, but catching Alex's eye meaningfully.

He could see she was trying to stay relaxed. Lilly had spoken out loud. Not to him directly. But definitely so he could hear. She had changed her mind on whispering privately to her mother and actually spoken aloud.

He watched. He couldn't not. There was something mesmerizing about observing the pair of them together. As if Lisa wasn't enough, the girl was enchanting. Especially when she spoke.

"I'm going to do what?" he asked, trying to encourage her to talk again.

Lilly gave him one of her crooked quirks of a smile and then ran, arms stretched out wide as if she might fly.

"Catch a fish!" she called out.

"Huh." He stared at the water, feeling the quiet lull as he stared into it. "If you don't catch *me* with the hook first."

He looked sideways at Lisa. It didn't seem to matter when he looked at her, what time of the day, there was always a trace of a smile turning the edges of her mouth upward. But today there was a big one.

Lilly skipped off.

"You were great with her today, Alex." She turned to him, suddenly serious.

"You saw us?"

She nodded. "It means a lot to me."

He didn't speak as she paused. He recognized it now—she was thinking about William, or the past, or worrying about Lilly.

"And did you notice her speaking just then?" Her voice was low, but it thrummed with feeling.

He grinned. "I know."

"She always understood why Daddy was away, but since the service, since I told her, she's just been…different."

"Like with the not talking?"

Lisa closed her eyes. He wanted to reach for her. To cover her hand. Brush his fingertips over the soft smoothness of her cheek.

But he didn't. It had been a long, long time since he'd touched someone like that. Known what it was like to do something like that so naturally. So long since he'd had someone to care about him. Or vice versa. The army might have been a great substitute family, but it was all about control and order. What he'd missed out on were the casual touches and gentle love of a real family.

So instead he just watched. Absorbed her sadness and stayed still, immobile, unable to comfort her.

"I get it," he said.

She opened her eyes and looked at him.

"It's hard to talk sometimes. Just give her time," he elaborated. He knew that first-hand. Years ago he'd been Lilly. Deep down, after all he'd lost and what he'd seen, he still was that quiet child inside.

Lisa reached for his hand. Gave him the comfort that she herself needed. He almost pulled away, but the gentleness of her skin on his stopped him. Forced him to halt.

"That's why she likes you. Because you understand one another. Somehow," she added wryly.

He looked back out at the water. He guessed she was right. He did recognize what Lilly was going through. Maybe she sensed that.

When he turned back, Lisa's eyes were still tracing his face. Openly watching him. As if she was trying to figure him out.

"Are you still taking her to the therapist?" he asked.

"Next week." Lisa bent her knees up and moved to stand.

She leaned close to him, because she had to rise, and he felt it. Felt the heat of her body, smelt the faint aroma of baking on her clothes.

He turned away.

"I'll see you inside," she said.

Alex gave her a smile but stayed still.

"Come on, Lilly!" she called. "Time to come in."

But even as she called, pulling away from him, he saw the look on her face. Her eyes flickered when they settled on him. Something passed between them that he didn't want to recognize.

He dragged his eyes away. He was on dangerous territory here and he knew it. There was no room in his life for complications. His entire past had been complicated enough to last a lifetime.

She was a widow. Confused. Still in love with her husband. Definitely not the type of woman he would ever take advantage of. Ever.

He'd built a wall around himself for a reason. And he needed to remember that the gate was destined to stay firmly shut. He didn't want to love or lose again. Ever.

CHAPTER SIX

His head was pounding. Alex was fighting feelings of wanting to run, and others of wanting to stay in this cabin his entire life. Being with Lisa yesterday had affected him. Being the recipient of her warm gaze, seeing the appreciation in her eyes, had just made him feel like a traitor. So guilty. Yet he couldn't bring himself to tell her.

Then Lilly had kept talking all afternoon, forgetting her silence, and that had made him feel worried all over again.

He could see her walking down the path to him now, skipping over like she hadn't a care in the world. He knew otherwise, but it was wonderful to see such a lightness within her.

"Hey, Alex! Wanna fish?"

Alex didn't want to go fishing, but she looked at him with the biggest, most innocent gaze imaginable, and he couldn't say no. Just hearing her speak directly to him had him tied in knots.

"Aren't you sick of fishing?" he asked.

Lilly shook her head fiercely before reaching for his hand. She gave it a couple of insistent tugs. "Come on, Alex. Let's go in the boat."

He should have just said yes to fishing. Now he had to get the boat out and spend the next hour or more with the kid. He usually wouldn't have minded, but today—well, he just wasn't in the mood. But he knew what a big deal it was, her coming out and talking to him like that.

"Okay, go ask your mother and then come back out," He instructed.

She skipped off. He wished he could be more like her. Truth was, he *had* been her—in a way. He'd been the kid with no voice, the kid who'd lost a parent. Only he had lost both. Had gone from having two parents to none in a matter of minutes. So he hadn't had a mom to coach and nurture him like Lilly had.

Alex looked up as a whine hit his eardrums. Boston was sitting maybe a few meters away, his head cocked on one side, watching him. Alex let his elbows rest on his knees, staying seated on the step.

Even the dog knew he was troubled.

"You don't have to hang around with me," he said softly to the dog.

Boston changed the angle of his head.

"Seriously, you don't want to know my troubles."

The dog came closer, sitting so near he almost touched Alex's feet. But he faced away from him now. Had his back turned to Alex, his head swinging around as if to check he was okay with it.

Alex let his hand fall to Boston's soft back. His fingers kneaded through his fur. The motion felt good.

He'd always wanted a dog. From when he was a kid to when he'd dreamed of the life he'd never had while away serving. Now he knew why. There was something soothing about having an intelligent animal nearby who wasn't going to judge you. A dog who knew the comfort his fur offered and turned to let you stroke it. An animal who knew when to stay with you and when to leave you alone.

"I don't know if it's harder being here, or harder thinking about leaving," Alex mused.

Boston just leaned on him. Alex liked this kind of conversation. The dog wasn't going to think badly of him. He was just going to listen. But it was true. He'd run from this kind of life, stayed away for this very reason for so long, yet here he was starting to think about what he'd sacrificed for being scared.

Lilly appeared. Her tiny frame a blur of pink clothing against the green of the surroundings. She raised her little hand in a half-wave as she ran back toward him.

Boston wagged his tail. It thumped Alex's foot.

"What did your mom say, kiddo?" he asked.

Lilly grinned. "She said to stop bothering our guest, but if he asked me I could go."

Alex laughed. She never failed to lift his mood, even if he didn't want her to. "I won't tell if you won't."

Lilly wriggled over to him and grabbed hold of his leg.

He was getting too attached to these two beings, not to mention the third one inside the house, and it scared him. But he felt happy. Actually happy. And it wasn't an emotion he felt often, so he wasn't going to turn his back on it. Not yet.

Lilly sat in the boat as Alex hauled it. She looked like a queen sitting in residence as he labored it over to the water.

"Faster, Alex!"

He gave her his most ferocious look, but she just laughed at him. It made him laugh back—a real laugh, the belly-ache kind of stuff. Until he tripped over as Boston launched himself in beside Lilly, landing square in the middle of the boat.

Lilly's peals of laughter forced him to push up to his feet. Fast. "That dog needs to learn some manners," Alex grumbled. He looked over his shoulder quickly, but to his relief he couldn't see Lisa anywhere. It made him feel better. Not quite as embarrassed to have been felled by a dog.

"Can Boston come fishing too?" Lilly pleaded.

Alex was going to glare a refusal at her, but he knew it would do no good. The child who had once looked at him warily, with big clouds of eyes, closed off from him to a large extent, was now completely immune to his reactions.

"Does he have to?" Alex groaned.

Lilly swung an arm around Boston and hugged the dog tight to her. The dog looked like he was laughing.

Alex could see the irony of it. He was a tough soldier, a man who had fought for years on foreign soil, but here in Alaska the dog was head of the pack.

"Fine," he acquiesced.

She resumed her queen position, with Boston as her king.

Alex guessed that made him the peasant.

Alex eyed Boston as he sat, tongue lolled out, focused on the water. He didn't trust the dog not to launch himself straight out into the water if he saw something of interest, causing the boat to capsize.

"Careful with that line." He placed his hand over the end of Lilly's rod. "Hold it like I've shown you, and carefully cast it over."

"Like this?"

A surge of pride hit him in the chest. She'd finally started to listen. "Good girl."

The smile she gave him nearly split her face in half.

He grinned back. He hadn't spent much time with children, but this little girl—she was something else. Teaching her, talking to her, was so rewarding when she listened or followed his instructions.

"Now we sit back and wait," he said.

She fidgeted. Waiting probably wasn't her favorite part. For him, waiting was what he lived for. The sitting back, feeling the weather surround you, thinking, losing track of time, it meant everything to him.

For kids? It was probably the worst part.

The water lapped softly at the edge of the rowboat; the wind whispered over the surface, causing a tiny rock. Boston lay asleep, and Lilly had tucked up close to Alex, leaning against him to stay upright.

"Lilly, I want to tell you a little story about what happened to me as a boy," he said.

It almost felt wrong to make the mood heavy—especially when she'd only just stopped yapping to him—but he wanted to help her. Alex hated talking about his past, and usually never did, but this time he had to. If it meant he could do something to help Lilly overcome her fears and find her voice with others he needed to tell her this.

She looked up at him, her eyes like saucers. "Like a story?"

He nodded.

Alex kept his eyes out on the water, one hand firm on the rod. He swapped hands, putting it into his left so he could swing his right arm around her. He didn't want to scare her, or make her feel upset. He wanted to comfort her. Wanted to help her like he wished someone had helped him as a kid.

"When I was a boy—a bit older than you—my mommy and daddy both died." He gave her a wee squeeze when she didn't say anything. She felt soft, not tense, so he continued. "I was just like you, with no brothers or sisters, so when they died I didn't have anyone. You've got a mommy, but I had no parents at all."

He'd had great parents. The type who would do anything for you. But his life had gone in one fell swoop from happy families to sadness. From light to dark. That was why being here shook him so much. Because he felt responsible for ruining this little family as his had been ruined.

"So who looked after you?" Lilly whispered.

Her eyes upturned to catch his held such questions, such worry, that he didn't know what to say. He certainly wasn't going to tell her the whole thing. This story was to help her, not to get the lot off his chest. "Someone kind looked after me, but it wasn't like having my parents."

He felt bad, not telling her the whole truth, but the reality of being in care had been ugly. He'd come across decent people in the end, but foster care was no way to live life as a grieving child. It had made him hard. Steeled him against his pain. Made him feel like it was his fault he was there. Alone.

"The thing was, I was very scared. And very sad," he said.

He watched her little head nodding. "Me too."

"And, just like you, I stopped talking," he admitted.

She dropped her rod then. He scrambled to grab it. "Just like me?"

He passed her back the rod and waited for her fingers to clasp it. "Yep, just like you."

They sat there in silence, bodies touching. She felt so tiny next to him. So vulnerable. Alex's chest ached. The pain of memories that he'd long since put to rest was bubbling in his mind, but he had to help Lilly if he could.

"It was different when I wouldn't talk, though. Do you know why?" he asked.

She shook her head.

"Because you have a mommy who you can still talk to. I had no one. So when I stopped talking I didn't say a word to anyone. I had no one to talk to. You are very lucky, because your mom loves you and you can talk to her," he said quietly.

She sighed and let her head rest against his arm. "But I don't want to talk to anyone else."

"You talk to me." He whispered the words, conscious that maybe she hadn't actually thought much about the fact that she spoke to him.

"Something's different about you," she whispered back.

Alex wished her therapist could hear all this. Maybe to a professional it would make more sense. "Why? What's different about me?"

"You make me think of Daddy."

A hand seemed to clasp around Alex's throat. Squeezed it so hard he couldn't breathe. But this was Lilly. This was the child he was trying to help. He couldn't stall on her now. She was waiting for him to say something.

"Is it…ah…okay that I make you think of him?" he asked.

She gave him a solemn nod. "It's nice."

Damn it! The kid had pulled out his heart and started shredding it into tiny pieces. "So, when do you think you'll start talking again? You know—to other people?"

She shrugged. "When did you start talking?"

He didn't let his mind drift back to where it wanted to go. Couldn't. He had been *forced* to talk again. Forced to deal with the fate life had handed him.

Being picked on and bullied had been bad enough. But being the kid who didn't talk? That had made life even worse in the first foster home he'd been put in. But he'd been tougher by the time it came to the second home. Harder. He'd had to find his tongue again in order to stand up for himself, although he'd kept his voice to himself most of the time. Tough kids talked with their fists, and he'd had to learn that type of communication too.

Alex had gone all his life wondering what it would have been like if someone had genuinely tried to help him. Had talked to him and wanted to help make it right. The army had been like family to him up until now, but those men he'd served with had all had someone to go home to. They had been there for one another, and he'd known true support and compassion and camaraderie, but it wasn't the same as having a real family.

He let his arm find Lilly again and drew her close. It didn't matter how hard this was for him—he had to do it for her. "No one can tell you when it's the right time to talk again, Lilly."

She snuggled in. Alex's heart started pounding loud in his ears. Beating a rhythm at the side of his neck.

"When you see someone like your grandma do you want to talk to her? You know? When she talks to you first?"

"Yes." It was tiny noise, one little word, but it was honest.

"How about next time one of your grandmas or your Aunt Anna talks to you, you take a big breath, give them a big smile like I know you can, and think about saying something back?" he suggested. He could almost hear her brain working. Ticking. Processing what he'd said. "If you can't say anything, that's okay, but if you think hard about what you want to say back, and try really hard to say it, it might work."

"Will you help me?" she asked softly.

He put his fishing line between his feet to hold it and hugged her, tight enough to show he meant it. "I'll be here for you, Lilly. You just be strong."

"Aaaaggghhhhh!" Her squeal pierced his eardrum.

If he hadn't been so focused on Lilly, so consumed by his own dark thoughts, he probably would have seen it coming. The dog had leaped out of the boat, which now rocked precariously and tipped before he could do anything about it. Alex kept hold of Lilly, more worried about her than the fact the boat was turning over. They hit the water hard, but he still had hold of her. Had Lilly pressed tight against his chest, her forehead against his chin.

Alex instinctively started treading water. He could do it for hours if he had to. "You okay?" he asked urgently.

His eyes met laughing ones. Lilly looked like they were on some sort of adventure, not as if she could have drowned!

"Boston saw a duck!" she spluttered.

He followed her gaze. Sure enough, Boston was paddling fast towards a few ducks that were lazily swimming in the other direction.

He could have killed the dog!

"Mommy told you he liked ducks," Lilly laughed.

Hmm, so Mommy had. Alex shook the water from his eyes and swapped Lilly into his left hand, so he could use his right for swimming. He hoped for Boston's sake he wasn't feeling quite this annoyed when the dog showed up on solid ground.

What on earth...? Lisa almost turned away just to look back again. Why were they both soaking wet? She ran to get dry towels and headed out the door.

"What happened?" she called as she ran. Her heart was pounding. Talk about giving a mother a fright!

She watched as Alex gave Boston a dirty look. The dog was soaking wet too. Standing on the riverbank.

"Oh, no. Did he…?"

"Leap out of the boat and capsize us?" Alex was at least smiling, if somewhat wryly. "Yup."

Lisa laughed. She couldn't help it. She held out her arms to Lilly. "Come here, my little drowned rat."

Lilly scuttled into her arms and Lisa wrapped her in a towel. Then she passed one to Alex.

"He saved me," her daughter said proudly. "Alex grabbed me and swam me in, and then he went back for the boat."

Lisa smiled at Alex and mouthed *thank you*. He just shrugged. She turned back to her daughter. "Lilly, if I'd known you were taking Boston in the boat I would have been able to warn Alex. You know he isn't usually allowed in without a lead."

"Lilly Kennedy, did you forget to tell me that?" Alex asked incredulously.

Lilly looked sheepish.

"Off with you!" He ruffled her hair to show he wasn't cross with her. "And take that filthy mongrel with you."

"He's *not* a filthy mongirl!"

Lilly's struggle with the word had Alex and Lisa both in hysterics.

"Well, he *is* filthy, so off with both of you," Lisa finally managed to say.

They watched her run off after the dog, still wrapped in the towel.

"I think there's a hot shower with your name on it," Lisa hinted.

Alex grinned. "Good idea." He started to walk off.

"Thank you, Alex."

He turned back to her. "What for?"

She wanted to stay like this, in this moment, forever. He was so different, happy. Open.

"For saving her, for taking the time to talk to her. It means a lot to me," she elaborated.

"She's not exactly a hard kid to be around."

Lisa knew that. When Lilly was happy and talking she'd draw anyone in with her smile and chatter. These last few months it had been like having a nervous, tiny shadow of her daughter—a sliver of the fun little girl Lilly used to be. Her father had been away for a lot of her young life, but she had loved every minute with him when he'd been home, and had lived and breathed the excitement of having him return home one day for good once his term was over.

Now this stranger, this soldier, had turned up, and it was like Lilly's inner dragon had started to breathe fire within her again. Lisa couldn't thank him enough for that.

She stood and watched as Alex made his way inside. He might not say a lot, but when he did his words counted.

CHAPTER SEVEN

"ALL I'm saying is that it's hard to meet someone who'll take on a woman and a child," Marj said calmly.

"Great—thanks, Mom." Lisa scowled at the phone. "So you're likening me to used goods?" She scribbled down the final ingredient in a recipe and dropped her pen. Having her mother on speakerphone was not helping.

"Honey, you know I don't mean that," Marj protested.

Did she?

"I'm just saying that he must be a good man."

"Mom! For the last time, there is nothing—*nothing*—going on between me and Alex," Lisa said through gritted teeth.

"Well, what I'm saying is maybe you should give the guy a chance," Marj said.

Would it be so bad, moving on from William? Lisa heard a shuffle of feet and hit the hand control. She didn't want anyone else hearing this conversation. And she didn't want to discuss moving on. She still loved William. Period. What she felt for Alex was just attraction. A natural reaction for a lonely woman with a handsome man nearby.

"Honey?"

"Mom, I appreciate the support—I do. But I just need a little more time." She sighed.

She could feel his presence. Sure enough, within a handful of seconds Alex appeared in the living room.

"I've got to go. I'll come by soon." She hung up the phone. "Hi," she greeted him a little nervously.

He raised a hand in a casual wave. "Hey."

She tried not to let him see she was rattled.

"I didn't mean to interrupt you," he said, when she didn't say anything more.

"Don't be silly. It was just my mother. And I told you—the door is always open," she said in a rush.

He nodded. "She keeps a close eye on you, huh?"

"More like she's nosy. Her *and* Anna," she muttered. But she sensed he didn't really want to talk about her family. Well, that was fine. Neither did she.

"I'm about to head into town to run some errands," she told him.

Something crossed Alex's face that she couldn't put her finger on. Then his expression changed.

She waited.

"Would you...ah...like me to drive you?" he asked tentatively.

Lisa smiled. She'd love the company. "Sure—that'd be great." She watched as his face softened, like he hadn't known how she was going to react to his offer. "Let me grab a few things and we'll go."

"Am I okay like this?"

He looked down at his attire. She followed his eyes. What about him wasn't okay? Long legs clad in faded jeans. Tanned feet poking out below. Bronzed forearms hanging loosely from a fitted black T-shirt. Her gaze reached his handsome face and went down his gorgeous body again before she finally managed to wrench it away.

It was just an attraction. A natural reaction to a good-looking, fit, healthy male. It would pass, she told herself fervently.

"You look good. Add a pair of shoes and you'll be good to go," she said.

He wriggled his toes. She saw it. Which meant she was still

watching him. Darn it if her eyes weren't like magnets drawn to him!

"Let me get Lilly and my handbag and I'll see you at the car." Lisa forced herself to move. To walk away from him. She could feel him. Sense his big masculine presence. It was like when William had been home on leave, or between postings. The house had felt different. A feeling in the air. Only William had been a comfortable change. Solid, dependable. With Alex it was electric.

Lilly made the house feel alive, kept Lisa from ever feeling truly alone, but she couldn't deny that there was a sense of security, of strength, in a house when there was a man in residence. She dug her nails into her own hand. It was *William's* residence. Alex was just a visitor. Passing through.

But, wrong as it may be, there was definitely something comforting about having a man in her home. Even if it wasn't the man she was supposed to be sharing it with.

She looked at Lilly's closed bedroom door. There was a little thump and lots of giggling. Then there was a woof. Lisa guessed what was going on. Boston would be lying on the bed, on his back, legs in the air. His head would be settled on the pillows. Lilly would either have a bonnet on his head, socks on his feet, glasses on his nose, a blanket tucked around him, or all of the above. She treated the dog as if he was a living doll.

"We're going into town soon, honey," Lisa told her through the door.

"Can we take Boston?" Her voice was slightly muffled.

"Yes, we can take Boston."

Lisa let her forehead rest on the door. She owed a lot to that dog. Without him, Lilly would have been even worse. Would have been even more lost over William's death.

She heard a bout of giggles again. Lilly was definitely getting back to her old self. It was nice to have a daughter who was slowly filling up with fuel for life again.

"Get a wriggle on, girl. Two minutes!" Lisa warned.

Lilly didn't answer.

Strange as it might be, it was almost like things *were* getting back to normal again. Or as normal as life had ever been being a soldier's wife. Having Alex here felt right. In some ways. But deep down she didn't want it to be right. If she could wish for anything in the world, it would be to have William back.

So where did that leave her feelings for Alex?

Alex looked out the window as they chugged along. He didn't look at Lisa. He couldn't. Even though he'd intended driving her in, she'd laughed, told him to enjoy the scenery and jumped in on the driver's side herself.

Seeing her behind the oversize wheel of the baby blue Chevy had been bad enough when she'd waved him over before they'd left. There was something about her that just got to him. The casual ponytail slung high on her head, the way she wore her T-shirt, even the way her fingers tapped on the wheel to music.

He wound down his window and let a blast of air fill the cab. Boston straddled him and let his tongue loll out the window, nose twitching. Lilly wriggled next to him on the bench seat.

"Tell me again why Boston couldn't ride in the back?" Alex wanted to know.

Lisa laughed. Loud.

Relief hit him. Hard. Like a shock to the chest. He'd wondered if they were ever going to get that easy feeling between them back again. He'd missed it.

"Lilly won't have him in the back," Lisa explained.

He looked at the kid. She shook her head. Vigorously.

Alex pushed Boston back and wound the window up. He liked dogs, but four of them squished up-front seemed a bit—well, ridiculous. He went back to scanning the landscape. He might be biased, given the years he'd spent seeing sand and little else when he was deployed, but Alaska was beautiful. Incredible.

He'd dreamed of wilderness and trees and water every night before coming back to the US. Now he was here. In a part of the world that seemed untouched. It was the postcard-perfect back-drop he would have sketched when he was away. The idyllic spot he'd hankered for. As a child, he'd always dreamt of what his life could have been like, the kind of place he could have lived in with his family if they'd been around, and if he could have chosen anywhere Alaska would have made the list.

Even without Lisa and Lilly this place was perfect. *Although they sure did add to the appeal*, a little voice inside him whispered insidiously.

They'd only been driving maybe five, seven minutes before a stretch of shops appeared. They had an old-school type of quality—a refreshingly quaint personality. He'd driven into Brownswood this way, but he'd been so focused on following directions, on finding the Kennedy residence, that he'd hardly even blinked when he'd passed the row of stores. There was every kind of store here a person could need.

Lisa gave a toot and waved to an older woman standing on the street. She turned down the radio a touch and rolled down her window. "Hey, Mrs. Robins."

A few other people turned to wave. Small-town feel, small-town reality. The thought suddenly worried him. Was his being with her going to affect her standing? Surely she wouldn't have agreed to him coming along if she'd had hesitations? But still... He knew firsthand how small-town gossip started. And spread. When his parents had died it had been as if everyone had been talking about it. Pitying him. Whispering. But no one had stepped up to help him or take him in. They'd just watched as Social Services had taken him away.

Alex started pushing the painful memories back into the dark corners of his mind, like he always did. Just because he'd been doing better these past few days it didn't mean he was ready for this. Didn't mean he wanted to be seen or have to interact with anyone.

He did enjoy Lisa's company, he had to admit. That didn't mean he was ready to brave the world again, though. It had taken him years to learn how to force unwanted feelings down.

To push them away and lock them down. But now that he'd left the army after ten years he was struggling. Because he didn't want to be alone.

Having company again was kind of nice.

Lisa wasn't going to hide just because she had Alex with her. She had to keep mentally coaching herself, reassuring herself that she wasn't doing anything wrong, but it was hard.

These people had known her since she was a little girl. Known William since he was in diapers. Not to mention known them both together as husband and wife for a good few years. And the worry, the guilt, was eating at her from the inside. She cared about what people in her community thought about her. Plus she cared about her husband. She didn't ever want to be disloyal to him, or to his memory.

For some reason, though, it felt like she was.

But Alex was a friend. *A friend*. There was nothing wrong with having a friend who was a man. Nothing wrong at all.

Besides, she had been forced to start a new chapter in her life the day William had passed away. Like it or not, the residents of Brownswood were just going to have to accept that. She loved being part of the community, but would they expect her to be a widow forever?

Lisa focused her attention back on Alex. At her friend and nothing more. Pity about the flicker of fire that raced through her body when she looked at him. "Is there anything you need? Anywhere you want to go?"

Alex dragged his eyes back toward her. She didn't know what he had been looking at—maybe everything—but he'd seemed another world away in his own thoughts.

"Sorry?"

He *had* been another world away. He hadn't even heard what she'd said. "Is there anywhere you particularly want to go?" she repeated.

He shook his head. "Maybe a fishing shop, if there is one, but it's not really necessary."

Lisa pulled into a spare parking bay. It wasn't like they were hard to come by here, but she hated to have to walk too far. "I just need to do the grocery shopping, grab a prescription from the pharmacy, and take Lilly to her therapist appointment."

"I'll come help carry the groceries," he suggested.

She appreciated that he liked to be a gentleman but she didn't want him to feel like he owed her. Didn't want to need his help.

"Why don't you take a look around and meet me outside the store?" She pointed with her finger at the grocers. "I'll be about twenty minutes in there, and then I'll take Lilly to her appointment."

"Okay."

She watched as he gave Lilly a hand out of the cab, her petite fingers clasped in his paw. The one with the real paw whined, but stayed put.

"Won't be long, Boston." Lilly waved to her dog.

"See you soon, then," Alex said.

Lilly waved to him too.

Alex felt like a fish out of water. He hated that everyone he walked by would know he was new in town. It didn't look much like a tourist spot, so they probably looked at newbies as fresh meat on the block.

He decided to avert his eyes from the few people milling around and check out the shops instead. A hardware store, a small fashion shop, then a bookstore. He let his step quicken as he noticed a place across the road. Bill's Bait & Bullets. He crossed the road.

A stuffed moose head filled the window, along with an assortment of feathered varieties. He wasn't into hunting, but he loved to fish, and if the sign on the door was anything to go by then he was in luck.

"Howdy."

Alex nodded his head at the man behind the counter who'd just greeted him. He sported a bushy mustache and was a wearing a blue and white plaid shirt. He guessed this was Bill.

"You after anything in particular?" Bill asked.

Alex did a quick survey around the shop and eyed the rods.

"Looking to do a spot of fishing," he said, walking in the right direction. "Wouldn't mind a new rod. Or two."

The man rounded the counter and came back into view. "You've come to the right place, then." He walked over to the rods. "That what brings you here? Fishing?"

Alex didn't see the point in lying. Not when everyone around would be gossiping later. But he wasn't about to start telling this Bill all his business.

"Here to see an old friend." He left it at that. "I need a rod for me, and one for a kid. About so high." He gestured with his hands at what he estimated Lilly's height was. "Six, I think."

"Girl or boy?" Bill enquired.

He gave the man a stern look. Asking politely was one thing, getting nosy was another. It wasn't like fishing rods came in pink or blue. Bill was just trying to guess which kid in town Alex was buying it for.

"I just need a rod for a child," he reiterated firmly.

The man shuffled away, and Alex moved to look around the shop. It was at times like this he thought of William, about what he might be doing now if he'd survived. They'd spent a lot of time talking about what they liked to do, and William had always talked about his family.

When they'd kicked a ball around in the sand, sat back when there was nothing else to do, or lain side by side waiting for their orders, there had been nothing else to do but talk. And while Alex hadn't opened up much about his past, other than to tell William he had no family, his friend had reminisced about his little girl and his wife. Told him how he wanted to teach his daughter to fish and follow tracks in the forest one day.

So Alex felt good being here buying a rod. Felt right about doing something he knew William would have done, had he lived. He wasn't trying to take his friend's place—part of him still wanted to run when Lilly so much as looked up at him—but this was something he could do. In William's memory. This was the way he could help William's family through their loss.

Lisa found Alex leaning against the hood of the car when they returned for the second time. He'd long since packed the groceries into the back, after she'd met him at the vehicle with the bags, and he was now leaning with one foot against the front wheel arch and the other out front.

Lilly bounded up to him, then decided to give Boston, who was still inside the car, her attention instead. She'd coped well with the therapist. Now she was open as a spring flower, and Alex and Boston were helping to keep her like it.

"I didn't know if he was allowed out or not," Alex said, gesturing to the cooped-up canine.

"No, he isn't!" Even Lilly laughed at her mother's appalled expression. "He has a track record of stealing sausages from the butcher, snatching sandwiches—all sorts of things," Lisa explained.

Alex cracked a grin. It stopped her in her tracks. She'd seen him smile more than once now, plenty of times, but they were often sad smiles. Often haunted. This one was powerful. It showed off straight white teeth and set his eyes to crinkling.

"That the real reason he travels shotgun?" he asked.

"You've got me there." She smiled.

Alex opened the door and Lilly scrambled in. "She get on okay?" he asked.

Lisa gave him a thumbs-up. "Big progress." She crossed around the side of the car to jump behind the wheel. When she got in, it wasn't as crowded as she'd expected.

Lilly had crawled into Alex's lap.

Lisa's hand shook as she tried to put the key in the ignition. She turned on the engine. Then looked at Alex. His eyes were pleading. Torn between terror and something she couldn't identify. She was about to tell Lilly to get in her seat. About to take action. When Lilly's head fell against Alex's chest.

It nearly broke her heart.

Lilly had always sat like that with William. Lisa had always found them in the car like that, waiting for her to emerge from a shop.

And now she was sitting like that with Alex.

It was the first time since he'd come into their lives that she'd seen him fill William's boots. The idea of replacing William made her feel physically sick. But the ever-present thrum of attraction, of being drawn to Alex, quickly pushed away the nausea.

She met his eyes again. He didn't blink. Didn't pull his eyes away. The brown of his irises seemed to soften as he looked back at her. She watched as one hand circled Lilly, keeping her tucked gently against him. Lisa could see the gentle rise and fall of his chest. He still hadn't looked away.

She swallowed. Tried to. But a lump of something wouldn't pass. Lilly's doctor's words echoed in her mind, but she swept them away.

Something had changed between them. In that moment the goalposts had moved. It had been building up, simmering below the surface. But right now something had definitely changed.

She knew it and he knew it.

Alex wasn't pulling away from her daughter—but then she hadn't ever seen him truly pull away from Lilly before. They were like kindred spirits. The way they connected was—well, like nothing she had imagined, believed, could happen.

But he'd always pulled away from *her*. Always kept himself at a distance. Kept himself tucked away.

Not now.

Now Lisa could finally see with clarity that he felt it too. She'd been caught in his gaze too long.

Lisa placed her hands on the wheel. Her palms were damp. She put the car in gear, looked over her shoulder, then pulled out onto the road.

And then she saw her.

William's mother stood on the footpath. Watching them.

She raised a hand to wave to her, and cringed as guilt crawled across her skin. Swept like insects tiptoeing across every inch of her body. Brought that nausea to the surface again. Made her wish she could just stamp on the attraction she felt for Alex and go back to pining for William.

His mother raised her hand too. But Lisa could see the look on her face. It was pained and confused and upset.

Lisa thumped her foot on the accelerator to get away. She couldn't face her. Not right now.

She'd done nothing wrong, so why did she feel so guilty?

And why did she feel like nothing was ever going to be the same ever again?

She glanced over at Alex, taking her eyes from the road for a nanosecond. Lilly was still tucked against him. Boston had his head resting against his leg.

Could she really ever be with another man? William had been her one and only lover. The only man in her life. Her high-school sweetheart and best friend. The only man she'd ever wanted.

Did thinking about Alex romantically make her a bad person? She hoped not. Because there was no chance she could ignore Alex.

Not a chance.

She knew that now. And she didn't have the strength to fight it much longer.

No matter how much it was tying her in knots.

CHAPTER EIGHT

LISA couldn't look at Alex. She got the feeling he felt the same.

As soon as they'd arrived home he'd carried the groceries in for her, placed them in the kitchen, then made for the door. He hadn't even spoken to Lilly.

Lilly had fallen asleep against him on the short drive home, waking only when Lisa had taken her from his arms and carried her inside. She was still napping now.

Lisa poured herself a cup of strong, sweet tea.

She hadn't lied to Alex earlier, Lilly's therapy session had gone great. Lilly had smiled, drawn happy pictures, and nodded in answer to the questions the therapist had asked. She hadn't spoken, but she'd communicated in the way the doctor had asked her to. Through creative expression.

But at the end the doctor had called Lisa aside. She'd told her that Lilly was making a sudden burst of progress, and asked about Alex. Lilly had drawn pictures of him—a large man standing beside them. A man with a smile. Which meant he was both important to her and a current source of happiness.

The doctor had pointed out that she'd drawn a family picture. With Alex cast as the dad.

It was fine. Lisa could deal with that image in theory. But the doctor had cautioned her that Alex leaving at any stage, for whatever reason, might cause Lilly to go back, to retreat further into a state of grieving.

Lisa didn't even know if Alex had been officially discharged from the army. For all she knew he might only be back for a few months or so before he was redeployed somewhere millions of miles from Alaska. And he was only staying here for another—what?—two weeks? Would they just try to go back to normal and forget he'd ever existed once he left?

The very thought of him going back to the place that had taken William from her made her sick to her gut. But soldiers were soldiers, and they went where they were needed. She'd been a patriot all her life, and just because William had been one of the casualties of war it did not mean she had any right to want Alex not to go back. Or even to think it.

But the thought of him leaving worried Lisa, regardless of where it was he might go. She could ask him to leave now, before they became too attached to each other, but that could do Lilly as much harm as losing him in a week or more. She could explain that because he was a friend of Daddy's he had to go back to his own house, but did she really need to burst that bubble now if Lilly honestly thought he was staying for longer? Did she even understand that he wasn't here for good? Lisa was struggling with the idea herself.

She rubbed at her neck. The base of it seemed to hold all her stress these days. It was worry. She knew that. Her neck had prickled ever since... Well, she was going to stop thinking about that. About Alex. Every time she did it reminded her that she was a widow, and she didn't need a fresh wave of guilt on her conscience. Thinking about him didn't mean she was cheating. Didn't make her disloyal. Surely?

Seeing William's mother had given her a good enough dose of that.

Lisa looked around the kitchen. She could bake. That always made her feel better. But she'd already finished creating her recipes and ideas for the book. What she needed was a break. Plus that reminded her that she actually had to send her work to her editor.

The house was silent. Birds cawed in the trees outside, their

Send For
2 FREE BOOKS
Today!

I accept your offer!

Please send me two free Harlequin® Romance novels and two mystery gifts (gifts worth about $10). I understand that these books are completely free—even the shipping and handling will be paid—and I am under no obligation to purchase anything, ever, as explained on the back of this card.

About how many NEW paperback fiction books have you purchased in the past 3 months?

❑ 0-2
FDGV

❑ 3-6
FDG7

❑ 7 or more
FDHK

❑ I prefer the regular-print edition
116/316 HDL

❑ I prefer the larger-print edition
186/386 HDL

Please Print

FIRST NAME

LAST NAME

ADDRESS

APT.#   CITY

STATE/PROV.   ZIP/POSTAL CODE

Visit us online at www.ReaderService.com

Printed in the U.S.A. ▲ ® and ™ are trademarks owned and used by the trademark owner and/or its licensee.

© 2010 HARLEQUIN ENTERPRISES LIMITED. ▲ Detach card and mail today. No stamp needed.

H-R-07/11

noise filtering in. The sun let its rays escape in through the window, hitting the glass and sending slivers of light into the room.

What was Alex doing? She couldn't hear him, so he obviously wasn't working on the cabin.

She got up. Her feet seemed to lead her on autopilot toward the door. There was something forbidden about what she was doing. But she didn't stop. Just seeking him out felt like she was prodding a sleeping tiger.

It wasn't like she'd never gone out looking for him before, but today was different. Today she was haunted by the look in his eyes earlier in the car. Today she was a woman thinking about a man. Today she was fighting the widow who loved her husband still. Today she just wanted to be a woman who happened to like a man.

Lisa stopped before stepping outside to check her hair. She ran her hands across it, making sure her ponytail was smooth. She pressed her hands down her jeans and fiddled with her top.

She had no idea what she was doing. Why she was looking for him. But she had to see him. Had to prove to herself that there had been something between them in the car today. Something she wasn't imagining. Something that was worth feeling guilty over.

She followed the beaten path through the short grass and let her eyes wander out over the water. He was nowhere to be seen, but the lake calmed her as it always did.

Maybe that was why Alex had chosen to stay? Because he'd taken one look at that water and known he wanted to see it every morning when he woke up. She didn't dare wish that she'd been a reason factored into his decision.

Lisa gulped. Hard.

The door was ajar. Was he in there?

Her feet started walking her forward again. They didn't stop until she was at the door of the cabin, and still they itched to move.

She didn't know why, but she didn't call to him. Didn't tell him she was there. She didn't know why she was even seeking him out. She nudged the door open and took the final step inside. Her eyes found his straight away.

It was her who wanted to flee this time.

She looked into his face. Tried to ignore the fact that he was shirtless. That his tanned stomach with its tickle of hair was staring straight at her.

He remained wordless.

They just stared at one another. There was nothing to say.

They *had* both felt it in the car. It wasn't just her imagining it. She could tell from the sudden ignition of fire in his eyes that he felt the same.

He stood up. It was like a lump of words was stuck in her throat and no amount of swallowing was going to dislodge it. Or force it out.

His body sported an all-over tan. Or what she could see of it at least. His arms were firm, large. In a strong, masculine way—like he'd worked hard outside for a lot of hours. She didn't dare look down any further.

She met his eyes and wished she hadn't. She'd never seen him like this. Never.

"You need to go."

His voice had the strength of a lion's growl. She felt told off. He had demanded she leave and yet she couldn't.

"Alex." His name came out strangled.

He stopped in front of her. So close that she could feel the heat from his body.

She was immobile. Glued to the spot. She raised her hand from her side, moved it palm-first toward him. She ached to feel his skin.

He caught her wrist in a vice-like grip before she made contact.

"No." His voice was still firm, gruff, but it was losing its power.

They stared at one another, glared. His breath grazed her skin.

She wasn't going to look away. Every inch of her wanted him. She'd never felt so alive, so desperate.

"Lisa, I can't—" His voice broke off.

She could see the torment in his eyes. He looked cracked open, yet so strong. Determined.

But he was as weak as her.

When she'd been with her husband it had been warm. Soft. Comfortable. It had *never* been like this. Attraction, intensity, punched the air between them.

His grip on her wrist slackened but she kept it still. He shuffled one step closer to her, their bodies now only inches apart. His lips parted and his mouth came toward hers.

She leaned forward until their lips touched. Just. He caught her bottom lip in the softest of caresses.

Lisa let her hand fall against him. Felt the softness of his skin, just like she'd imagined, beneath her palm.

He moaned. She could only just hear it. His lips still traced softly against hers. It was the deepest, most gentle, most spine-aching kiss she'd ever experienced. And still it went on.

So soft that she almost wondered if she was dreaming it.

She opened her eyes.

The six-feet-plus of bronzed, strong male before her convinced her that it was real. That *he* was real.

It was as if he'd felt her eyes pop.

He pulled back. Hard. Then jumped away from her as though she was some sort of danger to him. Pulled away like she was poison.

"No!" He belted out the word.

She was numb. Couldn't move.

"No." Quieter this time.

She let her face ask the question. *Why not?*

"Leave, Lisa. Please, just leave."

His voice belied the emotion tearing him apart. Guilt cascaded through her. She was the cause of it. Of his pain. Why had she done it? Come looking for him?

"Alex…" she whispered.

"You're another man's wife, damn it! Leave!" he barked.

She shook her head, tears forming in her eyes. Because she wasn't a wife. Not anymore. William was gone. *Gone!* She was no man's wife. The knowledge hit her like a blow to the gut. She was going to tell him that, but he looked torn. Grief-stricken. He wouldn't listen anyway. Besides, she didn't want to talk to him.

His back was turned. So she walked out. Kept her chin high as the tears started to trickle down her cheeks.

This wasn't fair. Life wasn't fair.

She still loved William. But she wanted Alex too.

Was it wrong to wish for both?

Alex watched her leave. He couldn't drag his eyes away from her if he tried. And he had tried.

It was like he was lost in her. Powerless to pull away from her. But she wasn't his. She could *never* be his.

Hadn't he already thought all this through?

His body had rebelled. She had felt so good against him. Lips softer than a feather pillow, hands lighter than a brush of silk.

He straightened and reached for his shirt.

Yes, he had already decided that she was forbidden. But that was before. Before Lilly had tucked up on his knee like a puppy. Before their afternoon out in the boat. Before Lisa had looked at him like that.

Before he'd let himself fall in too deep.

It was reminding him too much of what he'd lost. What it had been like to be a child with happy parents. And how much it hurt losing something like that. He'd long ago decided you were better not having it in the first place than risk losing it.

The last foster-family he'd been with had put a roof over his head and food in his belly, but he'd still felt like they'd just had him in order to collect the welfare checks. They'd never treated him like they did their own son. And when the other soldiers, his family, had pinned up photos of their loved ones Alex had never been able even to look at the crumpled photos of his parents. Which was why he'd never let anyone close to him since they'd died. Because he had never wanted to feel that way ever again.

Alex looked out the window.

He had to force Lisa out of his head. Just because he liked being here, liked feeling part of this little family, it didn't mean he had a right to be attracted to her. Didn't mean she had a right to be attracted to him.

All he knew was that he wanted her. And that she was forbidden.

It would take a stronger man to pull away from her again, though. And he didn't think he could be any stronger. Alex had fought it for so long. Thought he could go without love. Without family. Forever.

But the pain in his chest, the pain that had been there suffocating him for most of his life, told him he was wrong. That no matter how hard he tried to forget, to move on and not think about the past or what could have been, he would do anything for a family to call his own. To recreate what he'd lost. And that was why he hated the fact that William had saved him and not thought about himself instead. Because family was everything in this world. It was the reason why Alex felt he had nothing.

Now he knew more than ever how much he really craved what he'd lost. How much he wanted what could have been. And it was killing him that he was yearning for the family that William had sacrificed to save Alex's life. How twisted was that?

It was time to move on. Or at least to get this cabin fixed up as soon as possible so he didn't look like he was running out on them. And then he'd leave as fast as he could.

* * *

Lisa wanted to curl into a ball and never emerge. What had happened out there?

Oh, she knew. She knew because she'd been the one to go out there searching for him. She'd known that there was something between them, and she'd gone out there hoping to find out exactly what it was.

It had certainly been an emotional day.

First she'd had to deal with the therapist, not to mention her mother on the phone. Then she'd seen her mother-in-law in town. And Lilly had curled up on Alex's lap, and then... Well, she didn't quite know what had happened with Alex in the cabin. What it was they'd shared.

She only knew that they'd both acted on it.

And it had been Alex who'd pulled away. When it should have been her.

Alex. Just thinking his name sent tickles through her veins. Made them jump beneath her skin.

He was handsome. He was strong. And yet he was also vulnerable. So unlike her husband it scared her. William had been so together. So controlled. Yet at the same time like a wide open book. Alex was mysterious. Hard to read.

Yet sexy as hell.

She was beyond confused.

There were people who'd like her to be a grieving widow forever. Her sister was one of them. William's friends fell into that category too. She had no desire to be miserable and alone for the rest of her life. No desire at all. But then she didn't exactly want to move on yet either.

She thought of William's mother. Her in-laws were possibly the only people in her life who were allowed to make judgments. She wouldn't blame *them* for wishing she stayed a widow forever. She had been married to their only son. She was the mother of their only grandchild. Of course it would hurt to see her moving on with her life.

But even though William had been dead only eight months, to Lisa it felt like an eternity some days. And like yesterday at other times. Yet she'd hardly ever seen him. She'd been a single mom in many ways for most of their marriage. It didn't mean she hadn't loved him—she still did—but she wasn't going to be made to feel like she didn't care about his memory just because she was a little attracted to Alex.

Truth be told, if Alex hadn't come into her life she might have taken years to date again, let alone think about another man the way she was thinking about him. But he was here now, and there was something between them, and she wasn't going to let what other people thought get in her way. She was the only one to make decisions about her love life. And right now she didn't know what she was thinking!

She lay on the sofa and closed her eyes. It felt good. Relief washed through her as she stayed motionless. Her eyes stung from having cried, but she felt surprisingly okay. If she could just sleep it off maybe she'd feel better. Lilly was having a power nap, so why couldn't she?

Lisa woke with a start. How long had she been asleep?

She stretched out her limbs and combed her fingers through her hair before retying her ponytail.

Lilly.

Lisa hurried up to her bedroom and pushed open the door. She was up already, but Lisa knew where she'd be.

Less than a week ago Lilly would have been tapping her on the shoulder to wake her up. Now she wouldn't have had a thought for her snoring mother as she skipped out to find their guest.

Alex. She didn't particularly feel like seeing him right now, but she didn't have much of a choice.

She rounded the corner. Sure enough, there they were, standing side by side at the lake. Boston lay nearby, but he rose to greet her. The other two didn't bother to turn. Lilly might not have heard her, but she knew that Alex had. If he'd been a dog his ears would have twitched he was so alert.

"Hey, guys," Lisa said.

Lilly swiveled. She nearly took Alex out again with her hook. "Mommy, look what Alex gave me!"

She gave Lilly a beamer of a smile and went forward to inspect it. Now she had pointed it out Lisa could see she held a pint-size rod. Perfect for her little hands. "Wow! Your own rod, huh?"

Lisa acted like everything was normal, even though hearing Lilly talk in front of someone else still stole her breath away and made her want to jump for joy. But, just as the therapist had instructed her, she ignored it. For good measure she kept her eyes away from the lure of Alex.

Lilly had excitement literally dripping from her.

And Lisa couldn't help but look.

Alex still had his eyes trained on the water, his line out. But she knew he was listening. "I hope you said thank you to Alex, sweetie?"

Lilly nodded. Smugly.

Lilly turned back to the water and put the line over her shoulder. Lisa could tell there had been some practicing going on.

"Cast it back in the water like I showed you, nice and steady," Alex said quietly.

"Watch, Mom, watch!"

Lisa couldn't not watch, although half her gaze was focused on Alex. He stood with his feet spread shoulder-width apart, arms raised slightly from his sides. He looked as if he would be comfortable standing like that all day.

"Alex! Alex! Something's pulling!"

Lisa jumped at her daughter's excited train of words.

Alex calmly put down his own rod. "Stay still. Keep your hands steady."

Lilly did as she was told.

Alex moved to stand behind her and placed his hands over hers. Lisa couldn't hear what he was saying, but he was whispering in Lilly's ear as he guided her.

A splash indicated the line had emerged from the water, followed by an excited squeal from Lilly. "It's a fish!"

Lisa knew what would come next.

Alex helped her bring it in, then placed it on the grass. He worked to unhook it as they watched.

"Don't hurt it!" Lilly exclaimed.

Lisa tried not to laugh.

Alex looked confused. Lisa watched in amusement as his eyebrows formed a knot. "Aren't we going to have the fish you caught for dinner?"

Lilly shook her head. At rapid speed.

He sighed. "Shall we throw it back in, then?"

She nodded this time. A big grin on her face.

Alex threw Lisa a wry look over his shoulder—the first time he'd looked at her since what had happened between them earlier. "Here goes."

He let the fish go. Lisa knew as well as he did that it might die anyway, but Lilly looked happy.

"Bye, Mr. Fishy."

Alex shook his head in mock dismay.

"Let's catch another one, Alex!"

Lisa thought she could listen to her daughter talk to Alex all day. Now that she was speaking to him she'd probably never stop.

Lisa knew something was wrong the moment she walked inside. The light, happy feeling bubbling inside her from hearing Lilly talk turned off like a tap.

Something was wrong. Then she heard it. A soft rasp at the front door, only just audible. She went to see who it was. Her sister or mother would have just walked in. She knew it was unlocked because she'd been too caught up in her thoughts to go and lock it earlier.

Lisa swung it open. The person standing there took her breath away. It was William's mother.

"Sally." She tried to hide her discomfort. "I…ah…it's good to see you."

The woman looked like a shell of a human. Her eyes had lost the freshness they'd once enjoyed. Lines tugged at the corners of her eyes where before her skin had been seamless.

Lisa knew how she felt. That hollow feeling, and then the desperate barrage of grief-stricken emotion. It was what she'd experienced herself when the messenger had come. It still gripped her late in the night, when the cold sweat on her skin told her that William was gone for good.

For Sally, the torment was written all over her face. She would never see her son again. Just like Lisa was never going to see her man again. But at least Lisa had Lilly to keep her going every morning when she held her in her arms.

Sally had her husband and her grandchild, but she had lost her only son.

Lisa ignored the guilt tugging within her belly. She wasn't trying to replace William—she could never do that—but today she had for the first time wondered if she could actually start over. Give herself another chance while at the same time not forgetting William. The guilt she felt now told her that maybe she wasn't ready yet. She might never be. Not entirely. But Alex had at least made her want to find out.

"Lisa, I'm sorry, I shouldn't have come," the other woman said tremulously.

Lisa stepped forward and pulled Sally into her embrace. "Yes, you should have."

They stood like that, wrapped in one another's arms, not moving.

"Sally, about before—" Lisa started.

The older woman stepped back and dabbed at her eyes with a handkerchief, a shaky smile on her face.

"You've nothing to explain," Sally insisted.

Lisa appreciated not being judged. "But I want to."

"It's just—well, people were talking. After seeing you. I wanted to know for myself," Sally said.

Lisa nodded. Oh, she knew how the town would be gossiping. They'd all have her dripping in black and a grieving widow until the end of her days if they could. But deep down she didn't care about them. Or anyone. Except her husband. And her family. And Sally was family, even if they were no longer connected by her marriage.

She linked her arm with Sally's and led her into the kitchen. "There's someone outside who I want you to see."

Sally looked confused.

"The man you saw me with." She paused as Sally's face took on a hue of uncertainty. "He is—was—a friend of William's."

She sensed relief in the other woman. Her shoulders suddenly didn't appear so hunched, so shriveled.

"He served with William. He's just returned home."

Sally's eyes looked hopeful. "Was he with William...at the end?"

"Yes."

Sally closed her eyes as Lisa held her hands even tighter.

"He's—well, he's troubled," she warned. "He doesn't like talking about what he saw over there."

Sally nodded. "Not many do." She gave Lisa a brave smile. "Not like our William did."

"I do want you to meet him,' Lisa reiterated. "But I want the time to be right."

"I understand," Sally said.

Lisa beckoned with her hands and stood up. Sally did the same and Lisa put her arm around the older woman and led her to the window.

Alex was visible. He was still with Lilly. They stood side by side at the edge of the lake.

"Are you two...ah..." Sally cleared her throat "...seeing one another?"

Lisa shook her head slowly. "No." She wasn't lying. There was nothing between them. Yet. If there was she would have said. But she *had* thought about it. Had wondered if there was any chance of something happening for real between them. Although after his reaction earlier...

Sally leaned into her. "Do you want there to be?"

Lisa didn't answer straight away. She'd known this woman for years. She'd been a fantastic mother-in-law. And she wasn't about to start lying to her—not when she'd never done it before.

"I think so." It felt strange saying it, but it was the truth. If there was a way to be loyal to William, keep her family happy, *and* attempt to develop something with Alex—well, she would do it. The thought made her bones rattle.

Sally started to nod, and as she did she also started to cry. Tears pooled in Lisa's eyes too, but she fought them. She didn't want to hurt this woman—or herself.

"Would William approve of you being with him, do you think?" Sally asked.

Lisa knew the answer to that. She'd wondered that in the night. This afternoon too. Hadn't wanted to think about it, but she knew the answer without even pondering on it. William had been kind, open and loving. He would have wanted her to be happy.

"Yes." She hugged Sally tighter. "In his absence, I can honestly say that, yes, he would." Tears stung her eyes once more.

Sally still had her gaze trained on Alex. Lilly was leaning against him, like she was tired. "Then you have my blessing," she said quietly.

Lisa's shoulders almost rose to the ceiling. It was as if the heaviest of weights had been removed. Not because she definitely wanted to move on, or because she was sure about her feelings for Alex yet, but because it was one less thing she had to battle with. To feel guilty about.

"You know this doesn't mean I didn't love William," Lisa said urgently.

Sally turned damp eyes on her and put both hands on her

shoulders. "You were a good wife to him, Lisa. And we'll always love you."

The Kennedys were good people. But she'd never thought they could be so understanding. Not when she wasn't even sure about her feelings or whether she forgave herself for being attracted to someone else so soon.

"Would you like to come around on Sunday night? That will give me some time to…get some things organized," Lisa suggested.

"That would be great. Why don't you come to our place, though?" Sally offered.

Lisa wasn't sure how happy Alex would be about going, but she knew he'd make the effort. Maybe it would help him. Just maybe. And maybe it would also help her to finally figure out her feelings.

CHAPTER NINE

"WHAT do you say we go for a picnic today?"

Lisa looked up at Alex as she asked the question. He was sitting eating his breakfast. There were kitchen facilities out in the cabin, but Lisa had made a habit of asking him in for meals.

She liked the company—although he was nothing like William had been in the mornings, up before her, chatting up a storm, planning their day. She enjoyed Alex's company even if he was quiet. There was something about him, about his presence, that appealed to her. And he seemed to have forgiven her for seeking him out and precipitating their kiss yesterday.

Besides, there was no fridge out there, so he wasn't exactly going to keep milk, was he?

He chewed his toast. Thoughtfully. Lilly sat beside him, slurping at a bowl of cereal.

"Okay," he said.

Lisa stifled her laugh. He didn't get a very good score in the enthusiasm stakes. "I thought it would be nice to take a walk through the National Park. Boston can come with us on a lead."

Alex nodded. This time he didn't take so long to make a decision. It was like something had changed between them yesterday. Even after what had happened, they seemed to have silently moved on. He was more open. Different. And there was even more of a closeness between him and Lilly. Lisa could sense it. Perhaps they'd been talking more than she realized?

"Do you walk the same track each time?" he wanted to know.

Lisa enjoyed a ripple of excitement as she saw she'd piqued his interest. One of the reasons this property was so special to her was its connection to nature. It was a nice feeling to think he was going to share it with her.

"I'll meet you outside the cabin in an hour. You'll find out all about it then."

Alex went back to eating his toast and Lisa rifled through the fridge for the makings of the picnic. Lilly loved going on excursions, but she knew better than to rush off empty handed.

And it helped keep her mind off Alex. There was a spark, a flame that traveled between them when they were close, but he was so hard to get to know. The barrier he'd built around himself was made of something strong.

Lisa loved being outdoors. Loved hanging out with her daughter and enjoying the weather. She hoped Alex would too. Anything to bring him a little further out of his shell. Right now it was like they went two steps back for every one forward.

She wanted to know more about the demons he fought. She wanted to know if she could help him. Yesterday, she'd never thought it would be possible. Not when she still loved William so much. Not when Alex had pushed her away.

Now she was wondering if maybe, just maybe, something real could develop between the two of them. If they both took a big leap of faith.

Lilly was dancing along the edge of the river as Lisa attempted to haul the rowboat from its makeshift house. She heaved hard, but it was only moving an inch at a time.

"Hey!"

She turned at the sound of the voice and watched as Alex crossed the yard.

"Let me get that."

She stood back. Grateful. She didn't much mind rowing it, and it usually wasn't so hard to get it out, but it had sat dormant since William's last visit home and then gone back wet the other day after it had been capsized. She should have told Alex to just leave it out.

He made it look easy, though. Alex hauled it behind him, the thick rope looped over his shoulder.

"You want to launch here?" he asked.

"Perfect."

She passed Alex two packs, which he placed in the boat. Then he reached for Lilly.

"Need me to do anything else?" he said.

"Grab the dog." That was the part she hated. Boston usually leapt and toppled them out, or she had to pick him up already wet.

Alex chased the dog and tackled him. "Come here, you filthy mongrel!"

Lilly laughed. Alex was trying his best to look stern.

Lisa decided not to point out how dirty Alex's T-shirt had become. He manhandled Boston into the boat, but the dog didn't seem to mind. He'd taken to Alex almost as quickly as Lilly had.

"Sit!" Lisa used her sternest voice.

Boston surprised her by obeying for once. She wondered if it was her command or the dirty look Alex gave him that had him sitting still.

Alex took up the paddles. "Where to?"

"I can row," she offered.

Alex looked her up and down before shaking his head. "I could do with the exercise."

That suited her just fine. She sat back with Lilly. Besides, it meant she got to admire him while he pulled the oars. Today was the first time she didn't feel quite so guilty about admitting she liked the look of him. Didn't feel quite so sinful.

"Head upstream. We go maybe ten minutes up, then get out to follow a trail," she instructed.

He started to row. She watched his arms flex back and forth. Her ten minutes might not even make it to sixty seconds, given the speed at which he was propelling them!

"Just watch out for ducks," she said slyly.

He slowed. Then gave her a pointed look.

"Boston tends to jump." She grinned.

"You think I don't know that?" he said.

Lisa laughed. "Just reminding you."

Alex shook his head and glared at the dog. "Not again."

Boston looked up at him like a sweet little lamb. Lisa knew that look well, and didn't trust him one bit.

"It's beautiful here," Alex commented, looking around.

"Take us in over there, by the outcrop," she said, pointing. He slowed his paddling and expertly guided them in.

Lisa reached out to catch the edge and tie the little boat to it. She looked back at Alex. He was holding both packs. She took one and strapped it to her back.

"Ladies first," he said gallantly.

She climbed out carefully, and then put her hand out to take Lilly. Alex helped guide her. Boston was long gone.

"I thought we had to have him on a lead?" Alex said.

"We do. He got away from me, lead attached." Lisa grimaced. "Boston!" she called.

He emerged, flying out from between the trees, and came to a flying halt at Lilly's feet. Lisa grabbed him by the leash.

"Want me to take him?" he asked.

She threw Alex a grateful look. "Please."

They walked along in a comfortable silence that strangely made her feel closer to Alex than ever before. Lilly skipped behind them and inspected spiders' webs and bugs attached to the trees. Lisa kept up a steady pace, which had her lungs blowing after a while, but she didn't give up. Alex looked like he hadn't even walked an inch. His breathing was steady. No sweat. Just loping along. It was driving her crazy. Maybe she needed to do some army-style training to get her body up to speed.

He looked like he was chewing something over in his mind. She didn't pry. From what she'd seen of him so far, he needed to walk it off. Think. Not feel pressured. And he seemed relaxed despite it.

Lisa had already learnt the hard way not to expect too much in the conversation stakes. She was a compulsive talker, so it wasn't easy, but she could appreciate his pain. The way she felt about William wasn't exactly something she knew how to talk about. What he was feeling she guessed was on par with her pain.

"Tell me about Lilly."

Just when she thought he'd gone and lost his tongue, Alex surprised her by talking.

She slowed down. Lilly had fallen behind anyway. So much for a punishing pace! If she went any faster she'd lose her own child.

"What does her therapist think about her progress?" he asked.

She still hadn't figured out why he had bonded so well with Lilly. What it was in her that resonated with him. Why she'd chosen him to talk to after all these months. Lisa was too scared to ask either of them in case she rocked the boat. But what was it that her daughter's eyes had seen that had made her want to connect with him so strongly?

"That she's doing okay, but she's taken William's death incredibly hard," Lisa told him.

He stopped. His hand fell to Boston's head as he looked back at Lilly.

"Has she been prescribed any medication?"

Lisa thought that was an odd question for him to ask. "No. There were things offered initially, but one school of thought says time and routine is enough. I'd rather go for the non-medicated option."

"Good."

Good? What did he know about therapists and medication?

Did he go to one himself? If only she was brave enough to ask him.

"You're lucky to have a therapist in a town this size," he commented.

Yes, they were. "She travels in every other week. Does the rounds of a few small towns."

She sensed Alex had moved on. He seemed focused on the path ahead now.

"Where do you want to stop?" he asked.

"We keep following this path, not much further, then there's a small pond and a clearing. A few picnic tables."

"Mind if I run ahead?"

Boston looked ready to go too. "Go for it," Lisa said.

He surged into action. A steady rhythm that he seemed to find from his first stride.

She couldn't steal her eyes away.

His calves were bare, shorts ending just above his knees. His back stayed straight. Then he disappeared.

Alex waited for them at the clearing. The run had done him good. Boston lay sprawled out beside him, still panting.

Lilly came into view first, followed by her mother.

They were a pair, those two. Lilly had her hair tied into pigtails, but a handful of the hair from each had escaped. She gave him her usual grin and collapsed beside him. Lisa—well, he didn't even want to look at her too closely.

"Have you seen anything yet?" Lilly asked him.

He wasn't sure what she meant. Should he be keeping an eye out for something in particular?

"Mommy always says to keep your eyes peeled for moose and bear and caribou and elk and even wolves!" Lilly elaborated.

Lisa was shaking her head.

"Well, that's one very informed mom you have there," Alex teased.

Lilly smiled proudly.

"Let's have this picnic before any of the above find our stash, shall we?" Lisa said.

Alex ignored the niggle in his chest as Lilly sat beside him and Lisa fiddled with the food. Getting too close to these two would mean more pain. Emotions that he couldn't deal with again. So why did he suddenly feel prepared to risk his heart for the first time since his parents had died?

They sat on a rug beneath scarcely waving branches as sunlight filtered through to warm their skin. Lisa was conscious of Alex's leg close to her own. So conscious that if she as much as wiggled her leg her thigh could be pressed against his.

She hadn't brought up the kiss, but then neither had he. They'd skirted around the issue, and she had a feeling it wouldn't ever be spoken of if she didn't bring the subject to the table. Literally.

Right now it was like she'd been released. As if she'd realized that she could be happy again. That she could be a woman and enjoy the pleasures of another man's company without disrespecting her husband.

But she needed to understand this man. Know more about him.

"Alex, you've never mentioned anything about your family," she murmured.

Other than implying he didn't have one.

A wary look danced across his face. She recognized that look now. Knew it meant for her to back off. Fast.

"You don't have to tell me. I was just curious," she said reassuringly.

He lay back, his hands finding a spot beneath his head. Lisa held her breath. He was going to talk. She could feel it. To her it seemed like a major breakthrough. As if they were finally connecting. What they had, the bond between them, meant he could finally trust her.

"My parents are both long-dead. It's just me," he said tonelessly.

So there was a reason he'd never mentioned them. A reason he'd kept them close to his chest. "You lost them young?"

"Yup."

She drew her knees up to her chest and hugged them. Maybe if she offered him something of her own past he'd keep communicating. "My father died of a heart attack when I was pretty young. So then it was just me, Mom and my sister."

He propped himself up on one elbow. "You were close to your father?"

She gulped. It still made her feel sad, thinking about her father. "Very." She might have been eighteen when he'd died, but it had still hit her extremely hard.

Lisa watched Lilly where she sat with Boston less than a few feet away. She was sprawled out with him, stroking his fur. They often spent hours like that. "Where do you live, Alex? I mean before your term away where did you live?"

A shadow over his face told her she'd probably asked enough questions for the day. But she needed to know. Wanted to know more about him.

"California. Originally."

She nodded.

"But I haven't exactly had a place to call home for a long, long time," he admitted.

"That must be hard. Not having somewhere to go."

They sat silent for another few moments. Lisa looked up at the trees, her head snapped right back, and Alex plucked at the short shoots of grass.

"Alex, are you going to be deployed again?"

She sensed him tighten.

"No."

Lisa could have leapt to touch the highest branch! She had been fighting that question for days, hours, and to hear him say no was the best news she'd received in a long while. Relief shuddered through her. She didn't need to pine for another soldier. Not ever. Losing one was enough. She wasn't even sure if she could ever truly let another man into her life. Even Alex. She certainly could never, ever cope with losing another one.

He drew up to his full height and brushed off his shorts. "Shall we get back to the boat?"

Lisa didn't push him. There was nothing else she needed to ask. She put out a hand for him to help haul her up. He did. His hand clasped over hers and pulled her upright. His fingers felt smooth, firm against hers.

She didn't want to let go.

She was starting to read him. To understand him. To put all the pieces of the jigsaw together slowly. He might have stopped talking, but he hadn't closed himself off. His eyes were still light, open. He wasn't shutting her out. Alex's lips hinted at a smile. Hers were more than hinting, but she was trying to keep herself in check.

He's not going back. He's not going back. The words just wouldn't stop ringing in her ears. Did it mean she could let something happen between them? That if something special developed she could find room for both William and Alex in her heart?

She let go of his hand as he pulled back. Reluctantly. He started to scoop up their belongings and she helped him to pack.

What she needed was to keep him talking without pushing the wrong buttons. They'd covered enough heavy stuff for today, but it felt good to just talk openly without him being guarded.

"Do you cook?" Was that a silly question for her to ask, given the years he'd probably spent in the army?

"I do a mean lasagna, and that's it," he replied.

"One signature dish?"

He nodded before swinging a pack in her direction. A wolf-ish smile turned the corners of his mouth upwards in the most delicious arrow. "Just the one."

She'd bet it tasted good too. It had been a while since anyone had cooked her a meal, but she'd like to try his lasagna. Might even pick up a few tips.

"I'll do it for you one time before I go," he promised.

A drum beat a loud rhythm in her ears. She'd almost forgotten their being together was coming to an end soon.

"Come on, Lilly." She forced her voice to comply with her wishes. To not show him how upset she was.

Lilly stretched like a kitten, then stood up. She grinned at Alex. Lisa didn't miss the wink he gave her.

"Let's go."

Alex fought to keep his pace slow and steady. He liked moving fast, but he wanted to enjoy walking beside Lisa. He'd had fun with his army buddies, his makeshift family, but times like this were a rarity for him. Once he'd enlisted he'd volunteered for every deployment and opportunity he could to stay overseas rather than come back to America. Because he'd had nowhere to go, nowhere to call home.

When others had gone home for even a few days if they could, jumped at every opportunity to come back, he'd stayed away. When the army was your only family you didn't have anything else or anyone to turn to.

Which was why this felt so special. This was what he imagined all those men loved about being back home with their loved ones. Just walking side by side with another human being, with a woman who made you feel happy and light. He could only imagine what it would have been like to come home to his parents—to his own family, even. Children.

For years he'd told himself he didn't want that kind of life. That he liked being a loner and didn't want to risk losing anyone close to him again.

But maybe he just hadn't realized what being loved, being part of a real family, would be like. Just what he'd sacrificed by closing off that part of him to any possibility of finding that kind of happiness for himself.

"Why are we stop—?" Alex's sentence died in his mouth.

Lisa turned to him. She motioned him to step backward. *Bear,* she mouthed frantically.

He obeyed instantly. "Quiet, Boston," he growled, only just loud enough for the dog to hear.

Lisa watched as Alex wound the lead tight around his fist, twice, then reached down to half his height to gather Lilly up to him.

Lisa felt a tremor of fear run through her body, gather momentum, and then explode within her. She'd never experienced it before. She was usually so careful, so aware.

They were still edging away, and the bear hadn't noticed them. Not yet.

"She's fishing," Lisa whispered.

Alex nodded.

"She hasn't seen us," she added thankfully.

Alex pulled them away behind a thick cluster of trees before stopping. "But she knows we're here," he warned.

Lisa's body shook again. Did she?

He must have seen the question in her eyes. "She knows. She just doesn't see us as a threat. Yet," he clarified.

They could still see her. Only just. If Lisa hadn't been so afraid she would have found it beautiful. This huge black bear, female, flipping her paw into the water and expertly tossing fish out.

Lisa glanced at Alex. He didn't look at her, but just like the bear she knew he had seen her. He'd just chosen not to look back at her. Yet.

"We need to move. If she has young we could be in real trouble," he murmured.

Lisa agreed. But she wasn't volunteering to move. Not with the bear right there.

"Can we walk back if we have to?" he asked.

She nodded. "It would be tricky, but it's possible."

He looked uncertain.

"They feed often at this time of year," she told him. She was angry with herself for being careless and stupid. Her head had been filled with ideas of a picnic, and yet if she'd thought—really thought—she'd have known this was a real bear time of year. They were still hungry—plenty hungry—and they were always out fishing.

"I don't think she'll hurt us—not if she doesn't see us as a threat—but she might not take kindly to Boston if he starts to bark," Alex said.

They were in serious danger. And for the first time in all her years of being an Alaskan, Lisa was worried that another animal was going to sneak up on them while they sat in wait. That she was going to make headlines in the local *Herald* about a trio eaten by a bear.

Alex met her eyes as his hold on Lilly tightened. She might not have known him for long, but seeing the grip he had on her daughter made her realize that he'd risk his own life to save Lilly. That she could trust him to get her precious daughter to safety. No matter what happened, he wasn't the type to let anyone down in a moment of crisis.

Boston let out a low whine and she dropped to her knees to comfort him. She buried her fingers in his long fur.

"So we're just going to wait?" Lilly suddenly asked.

Lisa sucked in her breath. "Shh, sweetie."

"Stay quiet, Lilly." Alex pressed his lips tight together to show her. "Quiet as a mouse, okay?"

Lilly tucked her chin down to her chest. Her blue eyes looked double their usual size as she clung to him. Lisa wished she was in his embrace herself, being held safe, but she banished the thought. Now was definitely not the time to think about why she wanted to be in Alex's arms.

He gave her a nudge with his leg and indicated with his head. Lisa followed his steel-capped gaze and found herself wriggling closer to him. She stood against him, their bodies skimming, and she had no intention of moving away.

The bear fell back to the bank, on all four legs now, and looked around. She sniffed at the air.

Lisa's heart thumped.

The bear finally turned her nose down and loped off into the forest.

"Let's go—in case she heads back this way," Alex said authoritatively.

Lisa knew not to run, she knew it instinctively, but still she moved faster than she should.

"No." Alex's voice was no more than a whisper but it held as much command as a shout.

She slowed obediently.

"We need to move fast, but carefully. When we get to the boat I need all three of you in so I can push off quickly," he said.

Lisa understood. She was just glad that today wasn't one of those days when she'd elected to head out with Lilly alone. Although she never would have taken Lilly and Boston on her own this far. They only ever pottered around the lake in the boat or strolled down the bank close to home when it was just the three of them.

They reached the boat.

"In," urged Alex.

She took Lilly from him and he threw the dog in. They sat tight together as Alex pushed them out and jumped in. He took the oars from her.

"Hold that dog," he muttered.

Oh, she was holding him all right. And Lilly. There was no chance at all she was going to let go of either of them.

Alex steered the boat toward the little jetty. He had eyed it up the other day, and realized he should have tied it there all along instead of putting it back in the shed.

A shudder hit him as he finally slowed. They could have been mauled by a bear today. Actually mauled. Or worse. Thank goodness the bear had stayed put. He didn't want to think about what could have happened out there.

He didn't want to think about being responsible for losing

someone he cared for again. For allowing another person he loved to die on his watch.

His parents had died taking him somewhere he'd begged to go. William had died protecting him. And now he'd been close to losing Lilly and Lisa because he had been less than aware of his surroundings.

Alex leaned forward to catch the side of the jetty and almost collided with Lisa. "Sorry," he said quickly.

She flushed slightly, but he noticed it. Alex tied the rope and turned back to help his passengers out. Boston first, since he was moving from paw to paw, then Lilly.

He looked at Lisa, then offered her a hand.

She took it, but not before turning a smile his way that sent a *ping* straight through his skin. There was something about her, something that made him want to touch her and look at her and talk to her. But he couldn't. He was torn between want and guilt. Every bone in his body wanted her, craved her, but it was guilt, worry, responsibility that held him back.

"Thanks for what you did back there," she said.

He didn't know what answer he could give her. He'd done nothing. Just acted like any man would have. Looked out for a woman and her child. He'd just been lucky the bear hadn't turned on them.

"It was nice knowing you were there for us," she went on.

"Just doing what I had to," he answered.

She stepped out onto the timber jetty, then turned, her hand raised to shield her eyes from the sun. "Don't think so little of yourself, Alex. Not all men can trust their instincts like that."

She walked off before he could answer, with her hips swaying and hair swishing. Maybe if they'd met under different circumstances—if he hadn't caused her husband's death—then he'd have been able to act on his feelings. Maybe if he didn't feel like he'd already caused too many people close to him to lose their lives, then perhaps he could have given in to his feelings.

But he'd never have met her if he hadn't been the cause of

William's death, been there by his side when he'd lain there dying. He'd never have made his way to Alaska if he hadn't been fulfilling his promise to his friend.

And what a place it was. Wilderness to satisfy even the most enthusiastic of campers or nature-watchers, and water to soothe a man's soul. Or at least he hoped that would be the case. He had his pack in the car, ready to go camping, fishing—anything so long as he was with nature. When he moved on from here, getting to know the terrain was exactly what he'd thought about doing.

"Hey, Alex?"

He looked up. Lisa was walking back toward him.

"I might take you up on that dinner offer."

A grin tugged at his lips. He couldn't help it. "Yeah?"

"Yeah." She laughed and shuffled from foot to foot. "If you like you can cook up a storm in the kitchen while I send my book off to my editor."

He shook his head, torn between laughing along with her and crying out loud like a baby. This was starting to feel too real, this thing he felt for her. Far too real. Despite his inner struggle, despite knowing it was dangerous, he wanted it all. To cook for her. To be with her. To laugh with her.

He should be packing up and moving on, not coming up with reasons to stay, to be closer to them. Trouble was, Lisa and Lilly were getting to him. They were under his skin and it was starting to feel good.

CHAPTER TEN

THE smell of food hit Lisa's nostrils and made her mouth fill with hot saliva. She hadn't realized quite how hungry she was. She penned a brief message to her editor, then hit 'send'.

Relief washed through her like a welcome drizzle of sunlight on heat-starved skin. Her brain and her creativity were zapped. Energy depleted. For now.

Lisa was grateful to have Alex downstairs. Having William home had always meant a happy, relaxed household, but he'd never cooked. Not in all their years together.

She didn't exactly know what she and Alex had. She just knew that being cooked for gave her a tingle of pleasure.

Lisa went into her bedroom and changed out of her walking clothes and into a favorite pair of jeans and a soft cashmere sweater. She eyed a pair of earrings but decided against them. Alex was cooking dinner in her own home. It wasn't like it was a date.

She squirted a spray of perfume in the air and walked through it, then decided to brush out her hair before twisting and pinning it loosely on her head.

Another waft of cooking tickled her nostrils and she followed it down the stairs. This was just too tempting.

Alex could possibly be her favorite person ever—for now.

Whoever had said that the way to a *man's* heart was through his stomach obviously hadn't met her ravenous appetite.

* * *

Alex looked up as Lisa appeared. He liked the look he found on her face. Even though she was laughing at him. Part of him had put the garment on just to see if he could make her smile.

"I see you found my apron?" she said, giggling.

He looked down and shrugged. "Seemed to fit, so I thought I would wear it."

She slipped past him and sniffed at the air. "That does smell like good lasagna."

He wasn't going to deny it. It felt good. Cooking again felt good. Being in Lisa's company felt wonderful. Just talking to another human being without having to look over his shoulder. Without having to jump at every bang. It all felt fantastic.

Without wondering if he might have fallen in love with her too.

Enjoying her company was one thing, but it couldn't be anything more. Not when it was his fault her husband had died. He had to remember that.

"Anything I can do?" she asked.

He snapped out of it.

Lisa leaned against the counter, her palms pressed flat behind her on the stainless steel. Her tummy peeked at him, her top riding up to reveal it.

"No." He said it more firmly than he'd wanted, but she didn't seem fazed.

He forced his eyes back to the oven. He stared hard at the lasagna. *No* to being attracted to her. *No* to wanting her. *No* to anything that involved her in an intimate way.

He growled. A low rumble in the back of his throat.

"Sorry?"

Alex turned. "I didn't say anything." He tried not to cringe.

She looked puzzled, but she didn't press the issue. "Wine," she announced. "I can pour wine."

She reached for the glasses—he hadn't known where to find them—and he saw a glimpse of lightly tanned skin again. This time he swallowed the groan. The growl. Not wanting her was a fight his will was struggling to push back against.

"I hope you don't mind but I found a bottle. I opened it to let it breathe," he said unevenly.

She turned that supersize grin on him again. "You *are* domesticated, soldier. Who would have thought?"

He didn't know whether to be flattered or offended. He decided to go with flattered.

Lisa twirled with the glasses and set them down. Then she held the bottle in the air, looked at the label, and poured it. "So tell me—who taught you how to make this world-famous lasagna?" She smiled as she held out the wineglass to him.

He took it. But he didn't exactly want to answer. "Just something I've learnt somewhere in my years."

She didn't need to know that he'd sought to replicate his mother's signature dish as soon as he'd been old enough to cook, or try to.

"Ah," she sighed, before sniffing delicately at the wine, swilling it and then taking a sip. "Just what I needed."

He couldn't take his eyes off her. Couldn't stop staring at her no matter how hard he tried. For once desire was overpowering his guilt. The knowledge shook him. There was obviously a first time for everything.

Alex took a sip, a much larger one than she had, then forced the glass to the counter. His fingers were in danger of crushing the stem.

"I see you managed to keep Lilly entertained." Lisa took a few steps so she could look into the lounge at her daughter.

"I guessed I was being had when she told me you *always* let her watch movies before dinner," he said ruefully.

Lisa winked at him and swilled another sip. "She's already figured that you like to say yes to her."

"I guess."

Lisa looked back and watched Lilly some more. *"Lady and the Tramp?"*

Even Alex knew it was an old movie. "She likes the greats, does she?"

He leaned on the counter—close to her, but not too close. He could smell her perfume, the light, fruity spice lifting up to fill his nostrils. She smelt divine. And his willpower was so diminished it was non-existent.

"I think it's the dogs slurping spaghetti together that gets her." She looked at him. "That was what made it my favorite movie."

Alex found it hard to swallow.

"Are you sure there's nothing I can do to help here?" she asked.

He shook his head. Firmly. "Nothing at all."

Lisa shrugged gracefully, then gave in.

What he hadn't expected was for her to wiggle up on a stool and rest her elbows on the counter to watch him.

He found it awkward. Exciting. Knowing she was sitting there behind him. He also found it unnerving. He'd never cooked for a woman before—never felt so intimate with another human being.

"You sure look good in an apron," she commented as he bent over to peek in the oven at the bubbling lasagna.

He cringed again and straightened hurriedly. Did that mean she was looking at his rear end? Now he felt really uncomfortable!

Lisa watched as Alex moved about the kitchen. If he wasn't so nervous he'd look perfectly at home there. He kept himself busy, finding ingredients and chopping.

She liked to watch a man work. Make that *loved* to. And she particularly liked to see a man in the kitchen. Or she now realized she liked it. She'd never actually had a man cook in her kitchen before.

Only problem was that she was starving. Her eyes flitted over Alex's body, up his chest and to his face. If she had a few more glasses of wine she'd be tempted to admit she was starving hungry for more than just food.

Alex cleared his throat. She made her mouth shut. Any wider open and she'd have dribbled the wine right down her front. It felt naughty. But somehow so right.

"I think we're almost ready," he said.

Lisa dropped her glass to the table, then went to retrieve his. It was almost empty. She reached for it, and the bottle. Then she went back for the salad. She attempted to steal a piece of cucumber, but her hand froze mid-move.

"Huh-hmm." The rumble of his voice made it impossible to steal anything.

She looked over her shoulder. Alex was holding the spatula at a very ominous angle.

A giggle rang out. Lilly was standing by the table, watching them.

"I didn't take you to be so protective of a salad." Lisa said the words dryly, but inside she felt weak. Not witty at all.

"Out of the kitchen, woman. Out now," Alex ordered.

He hadn't moved or changed his stance. Lilly was still in hysterics.

Lisa put her hands up in the air like a criminal caught in the act. "Okay, okay. Guilty as charged."

Having a man in her kitchen felt as intimate as having one in her bedroom. It had been her private space for so long, her domain, and yet here he was, taking charge and looking so... at home.

It scared her. And excited her.

Butterflies started to tickle their wings inside her stomach. She sincerely hoped food would appease them.

"No laughing at your mother." She gave Lilly her sternest look before falling into the seat beside her at the table. Lilly ignored her, as she'd known she would.

Alex came over with the lasagna.

"Yum!"

Lisa met Alex's gaze as Lilly banged a fork on the table in

excitement. Lisa would usually tell her off for bad manners, but tonight she was less about manners and more about living in the now.

Would this feel more like a date if Lilly wasn't here? If they weren't in the house she'd shared with William?

Resolutely, she turned her mind back to the food. She needed to focus on safe thoughts. Happy thoughts. Like eating. Like her daughter. Like the weather...

Who was she kidding? It felt like the first date of her life, even though it was neither her first, nor anything resembling a date.

"I hope it's okay." Alex drew her attention back to reality. "It's been a while since I've made it."

"It smells delicious," Lisa said with honesty. She nodded at Lilly. "And this one doesn't lie."

Alex served Lilly first, but when he went to serve her salad she shook her head. He angled his. It was like they were speaking in a secret language.

Lisa wondered for the umpteenth time what it was they had between them. And she wondered exactly what had been said that day they'd been in the boat alone, before it had capsized.

It was no surprise to Lisa that Lilly won the dinner battle.

"She does usually eat greens," explained Lisa.

The look Alex gave her said *yeah, right*, but it was true. Although there was nothing usual about tonight, so she was throwing caution to the wind. For once.

Tonight she wasn't a widow. Or anybody's wife. Tonight she was just a single mother, enjoying dinner with her daughter and a friend. That was as far as she was going to let her mind go, for now.

She passed her plate to Alex and watched as he ladled it with lashings of lasagna and a pile of salad. Her perfect meal.

Lilly was already tucking in, despite how hot it was, picking around the edges. Lisa was ready to do the same. Anything to distract her from Alex.

"*Bon appétit.*" She raised her glass in the air.

He did the same, but they didn't clink them. Instead they watched one another. Slowly. Letting their eyes drink their fill. She didn't dare hope that he was thinking the same as her. Didn't even know what *she* was really thinking.

Lisa reached for the wine. "Another?"

"Please."

He looked away then, and it took her a long time before she could brave a look back at him.

Her toes were wriggling. Her tastebuds were alight.

"You're going to have to share the recipe for this tomato sauce with me," she said.

Alex tapped at his nose. "Family secret."

She felt the pain of that comment. That made him the last person to hold that secret. But it was the first time he'd made a joke like that. It felt as if he was, in a way, finally letting her see the true him.

"I could trade you for the secret of pink macaroons?" she offered.

He grinned at her. Really grinned. "Rosewater macaroons don't sound very manly. Besides, everyone can have your recipe. Your book'll be on the shelves when?"

"Maybe a year. Maybe longer."

He laughed. "My point exactly. You can't trade something secret for something that will be public knowledge."

"I'll have you know that my recipes are not available for *public knowledge*, Alex." She stared him down. "The privilege of that will set you back at least twenty bucks."

Lilly pushed her plate in. "Finished."

There was not a lick of pasta or sauce left.

Alex reached across the table and tickled at her hand. "Did you slip that to Boston while I wasn't looking?" he teased.

She shook her head. Her just-grown top teeth bit down on her lower lip.

"Promise?"

"Promise."

She slipped away from the table and Lisa refocused on Alex.

They sat there in silence, finishing off their meal.

"What do you say I put Lilly to bed and we go for a walk outside?" The question burst from her. It felt like a big risk, blurting that out.

Alex's eyes looked hungry. Eager. She couldn't mistake it.

"I'll clean up while you put her to bed, if you like?" he suggested.

"Deal."

Lisa didn't like the cook having to clean too, but it was only once. She didn't like putting Lilly straight to bed on a full stomach either. But sometimes rules were made to be broken.

Alex wasn't sure whether to sit, stand, or just go wait outside. The two glasses of wine had started to help, but now they were just making him even more nervous.

Of what? He wasn't sure. All he knew was that there was something about being in a space alone with Lisa that made him feel in equal parts terrified and excited. Exhilarated, almost.

He stood, awkward, in the middle of the room. He could hear her upstairs, probably saying a final good-night to Lilly.

Alex decided on the sit option. He dropped to the armchair. It wasn't as comfortable as the sofa, but it did the trick.

Then he locked eyes with William.

His whole body jerked.

The photo of William in its frame just stared at him with an empty gaze. Guilt stung his body once again, with the ferocity of a blizzard of wasps.

A noise indicated that Lisa was descending the stairs.

He closed his eyes, counted to five, then opened them, looking in the other direction. William was not going to haunt him now. Alex wasn't doing anything wrong. They'd just had dinner, they were now going for a walk, then he'd wish her good-night.

His thoughts might not be pure, but his intentions were. He knew his place, what he'd come here to do. That he had to be careful.

He *knew*.

"Hey." Lisa stood there, looking like an angel descended from heaven before him. Her hair was loose about her shoulders. All reason left his mind as blood pumped through his body.

Alex noticed her legs, slender beneath her jeans, and her arms, hugged tight by the jersey. He noticed everything about her.

He was in way over his head.

"Hey." He answered her greeting softly.

Sorry, William. He sent a silent prayer skyward. He'd dealt with guilt all his life. But now...now he just felt like a man who was attracted to a woman. Drawn to a woman like he'd never been before in his lifetime.

If he could have done it without Lisa knowing he would have turned William's picture face-down to avoid those eyes. For once he didn't know if he could control his feelings, his emotions, his desires.

The cool night air snapped at their skin. Even though it was spring, the evening temperature still fell. Lisa skimmed her hands over her arms.

They walked along the bank, where grass fell down to the water. It was magical at this time of night. The water endless, the moon shining her white light down low. Lisa always wanted to walk after dinner, but it wasn't something she liked to do alone. Wasn't something she'd ever thought she'd enjoy with a man again. Not after so many years of sharing it with her husband. Not after believing she'd never fall in love again.

With Alex, right now, it was perfect.

"Let's hope we don't come across any bears."

She laughed at Alex's joke. Sometimes he was so quiet, yet other times he made light of a situation and made her feel completely at ease. She could only imagine what he'd have been like had he not been haunted by war.

"Did you miss this while you were away?" she asked cautiously.

He slowed his walk so that he was just swinging one foot in front of the other at irregular intervals. She slowed too.

"I missed the feel of earth that wasn't sand. I missed the wave of trees, the smell of the country. The comfort of being somewhere no one wanted to take your life," he replied.

She closed her eyes. She had no idea what it would be like to be in active combat, and she didn't want to know. William had always tried to skim over it, tried to make her think it wasn't that bad, but the honesty of Alex's words was precise. Real. He was saying it like it was.

"You never did say how long you were over there?"

He didn't hesitate. "I volunteered for back-to-back tours."

She looked out toward the water. It sang to her like a lullaby. Did it have the same effect on him? "How did you do it, Alex? How did you stay over there?"

There was a raw-edged honesty to his voice. "I had nothing to come back to. Nothing to want to come home for. The army was all I ever had for years." He paused. "When my parents died there was no one to take me in. So I ended up in foster care. The army was my chance to get out. Make something of myself."

She had no idea what it would be like to be an orphan. To have no family to care for you. The thought, to her, was unconscionable.

"So why have you left the army after all these years?"

He glanced at her. "Because I couldn't do it anymore. I felt like I'd seen too much, been there too long."

Alex stepped closer to the water. Closer to its silky depths.

She watched him. The breeze sent another shiver across her goosepimpled arms.

She couldn't deny it anymore. She wanted him in her life. Wanted to reach out to him, to tell him they could have a chance together. That they had nothing to feel guilty about.

Lisa walked up behind him. She stood there, so close she

was almost touching him, before placing her hands one on each arm. They settled over his forearms—strong, muscled forearms that clenched beneath her palms. Her fingers curled slightly, applying pressure to let him know she wasn't letting go.

"Alex..." She whispered his name.

He didn't react. Didn't move. He just stayed still.

Lisa started to move her fingertips, so lightly they barely made an imprint on his skin, until he made a slow half-turn toward her.

Alex met her direct gaze with his own. His eyes engaged hers with such intensity she felt a flicker of something unknown unfurl in her belly.

"Alex." She murmured his name again, but this time her fingers traced a path up his arms.

He raised a hand to her face. Touched her with his forefinger, running it down her cheek, while his thumb nestled against her chin.

Lisa felt a quiver that ran the entire length of her body. The softness, lightness of his touch sent a tremor across the edge of her skin.

"Alex." His name was the only word she could conjure. The only word she wanted to say.

He acted this time. Didn't answer her, didn't say her name, but answered her with his body.

Alex crushed her mouth hard against his. His lips met hers with ferocity, so different from that first time their mouths had touched.

Alex's free hand moved to cup the back of her head, pulling her against him as if he couldn't fit her body tightly enough against his if he tried.

Lisa felt her way to his torso, then ran her hands up the breadth of his back, up to his shoulders and down again.

"Lisa." His eyes looked tormented, wild.

She took his hand, slowly, carefully, and turned. He resisted. For a heartbeat he resisted. Before clasping her fingers tight, interlocking his own against them.

They walked back to the house in silence. This time it was not a comfortable silence. Lisa could have cut the tension with a blunt knife it was so acute.

She didn't even know if she could be with another man. But she wanted Alex so much it hurt. He was never going to be William, but she didn't want him to be. All she knew right now was that she desired Alex. Period.

Alex wasn't sure he could do it.

Lisa reached out to touch his face, just with one finger, and he resisted the urge to pull back. To turn on the spot, flee, and never look back.

But Lisa's eyes stopped him. The soulful depths of them, the honesty and trust and worry he saw there, made him reach for her hand again. She only stopped moving to lock the door.

The click of it hit him in the spine. He was inside for the night, and he'd never felt more apprehensive in his life.

Lisa turned those eyes on him again. She was so honest he couldn't bear it. So trusting.

She was waiting for him to make a move. Waiting for him to do something to say it was all right. But he didn't know if it was right. Couldn't tell her that it was.

The only light that was on was in the kitchen. He let go of her hand and went to turn it off. Darkness set its heavy blanket over them. Only a hint of the moonlight that had guided them outside let him find his way back to her.

"Lisa." This time it was him saying her name.

He could make out the tilt of her chin even in the dark. So defiant, so brave. He also saw the light quiver that made it tremble. She was scared. Not brave. As scared as he was.

He let his lips find hers, then he kissed down her neck, deep into her collarbone. Forgot everything and just focused on her.

"Upstairs." She choked out the word at him.

It felt wrong, yet at the same time it felt so right. He stomped on his inner demons and trusted her. Trusted that they were doing the right thing.

"Upstairs," he repeated.

She obeyed.

Lisa wished she could take a tablet to quell her nerves. A lamp provided some light, but she would have preferred darkness.

She'd only been with one man before, and it had never felt like this. The quiver in her stomach was back with a vengeance, her skin felt like acid was dancing along the surface of it, burning the tiny hairs on her arms. With William it had been kind, comfortable. With Alex the intensity of her own desire frightened her.

Alex shut the bedroom door behind him.

She looked at him.

He looked back at her.

Then he crossed the room like the strong, determined soldier he was. His long legs ate up the carpet before he pressed into her and walked her two steps backward until she felt the wall touch her spine.

Alex's touch was like fire. His mouth found hers. His hands seemed to search every inch of her. He bent to trace her collarbone, her neck, like before, then nibble lower, so slowly it tormented her.

Alex dropped to his knees. He ran a hand down one of her legs before slipping her foot from her ballet flat. He did the same with the other.

His hands found a trail up her legs as he stood up slowly once more, his mouth back to press hard against hers.

"Are you sure?" He mumbled the words against her skin, his lips talking into her neck.

"Yes," she whispered, her back arched with the pleasure of his touch. *"Yes."*

There was an unspoken nervousness between them. But Lisa wanted this like she'd never wanted anything in her life before. Her skin was alive. Blood was pumping with adrenalin through her body as if she was about to plunge from a cliff for the first time.

Yes, she was sure. She wanted Alex. She could no more put a stop to it now than she could stop breathing.

Lisa didn't know if he was asleep or not. His chest was rising in a steady rhythm, and she could hear the soft whistle in and out of his breath, but she didn't know if he was asleep.

She didn't think sleep was ever going to find *her*. She was exhausted, mentally and physically, but sleep wasn't searching her out.

Lisa felt incredible. She was tired, but her senses still felt ignited. In a way she felt brand-new again. Tonight had been about being brave despite her fears, pushing through her own personal barriers and Alex's too.

Tonight she had said finally goodbye to her marriage. She kept William in a part of her heart, but accepted she could be with somebody else and not taint the memory of him. It was like she'd become a woman all over again.

She moved closer to Alex. Anything to feel his body hard against hers again, to feel the planes of his skin and muscles beneath her fingers.

"Go to sleep." He spoke without moving an inch.

So he wasn't asleep.

"Alex?"

He didn't move. But she knew he was listening.

"Good night," she murmured.

His grip on her arm tightened, ever so slightly. Lisa settled her head on his chest and closed her eyes.

She hoped he had no regrets. She didn't. And she doubted she ever would. Never in her life could she have believed that another man would touch her heart the way William had for so many years. Yet here she was, with Alex, knowing that maybe—just maybe—she had enough love, enough room in her heart and soul, for both men.

She didn't ever want to forget William. But she also didn't want to push happiness and love from her life.

Love might just have come looking for her, and admitting it made her feel a whole lot better. For the first time she didn't expect nightmares. Instead she closed her eyes with a smile on her face.

CHAPTER ELEVEN

THE smile she'd given him, the closeness of her body before she'd fallen asleep, had made Alex stiffen in alarm. Even more so than when he'd first set eyes upon her that day on the porch.

It had been dark, and he'd mostly had his eyes shut, but he had seen that look. Seen the way she'd been watching him. It wasn't right. Not with Lisa. He was meant to be giving her a hand with the cottage out of loyalty to William. What he'd done was inexcusable. Weak. Wrong.

As William Kennedy's widow, she was forbidden to him. If he didn't know better he'd think he was falling in love with her. Actually falling in love with a woman who was so very much out of bounds to him.

He should be banged head-first into a tree for even thinking it, let alone admitting it to himself. Love was not something he'd ever seen in his future. The life of a soldier's wife was no life for a woman, and now here he was thinking about absurd things like love. The only people he'd ever truly loved were his parents, and he'd determined never to feel like that again in his lifetime. Never to be in a position to feel grief.

He couldn't ignore Lisa, though, or the effect she had on him. It had kept him awake nearly all night, that smile of hers. Haunting him with its power. Teasing him with its honesty. Making him question himself.

He looked up at her bedroom, at the curtains still shutting

the early-morning light out. He should have stayed with her. Should have been there for her when she woke up. Should have nurtured her like she deserved to be the morning after making love to her.

What had he done?

His mind skipped back to the night before. He couldn't not have done it—couldn't have pushed her away.

But why?

He had resisted beautiful women before. Not often, but he had. So what was it about this one? What was it about Lisa that haunted his soul more than any horror image of what had happened at war? What was it about her that made him push the boundaries, disrespect his friend's memory, and go back on his vow to keep his heart guarded forever?

He didn't need to soul-search to locate an answer.

She was different because she was a real woman. Not just some girl he'd met on a night out. Not a girl who had the same idea in mind as him, which consisted of one word. *Fun.*

Lisa was the kind of girl most men searched for. The kind that you took home to Mom because she would please even the most demanding of parents.

Lisa was the type of woman you wanted to love. To see mothering your children. Lisa was the type of woman he'd always avoided in the past. To protect himself.

But he had no family to take her home to. He had no one. He wasn't the type of guy who deserved a girl like that. Especially not her. Not when he'd taken her husband from her, ruined her chance for a family life.

Even with William's smiling face watching him from the hall and framed in the lounge he hadn't been able to resist her. He couldn't control himself, stop himself, when it came to Lisa.

And now he felt even more guilty than before. She was not the type of girl you made love to and then left in an empty bed alone. He'd been foolish last night, and had acted like an idiot this morning.

If he'd had the courage he would have crept back up those

stairs and crawled in beside her. Pretended like he'd never been gone. Pressed his body into hers and felt the warmth of her as she woke from slumber. Held her in his arms and kissed her eyelids before they opened for the day.

But he couldn't.

She hadn't been his to begin with, and there was too much keeping them apart to pretend she was. Or ever could be.

They had no future. It was impossible.

He had to tell her the truth. That if it wasn't for him William would still be alive.

He'd slept with the wife of the man who'd saved him. What kind of thanks was that? All he'd had to do was deliver William's bag of items to her. Comfort her, perhaps, if he'd really wanted to do something helpful. But take her to bed?

That was just unforgivable.

He'd taken advantage of a widow. Of a woman he should have vowed to protect. He'd taken from her, disrespected William, and there was nothing he could do to change it.

Being here with them, being part of their lives, had drawn him in. He'd run from it his entire life and he didn't want to be part of it now. Couldn't. Not after what he'd done. Not after holding William as he died, with a bullet in his chest that had been intended for Alex.

His friend. The man who'd talked about his family, told him and everyone else who'd listen how much he loved his life and what he had back home. So how was it fair that Alex was the one here and William was buried in the ground?

He heard a noise in the house.

It was now or never.

Alex kept his eyes open to avoid the memory or war, of what had happened, and focused on the porch to keep from seeing William lying in his arms. Looking up at him that day. Talking to him with such love in his eyes despite his pain.

To stop seeing scenes of his childhood that had started playing over and over in his mind. Of his family before they'd been taken from him. Of what he might have had to come home to if they were still alive.

When Lisa appeared he was going to tell her the truth. It was what he had to do.

A smile lit Lisa's face as she walked. Last night had been incredible. Even her skin felt as if it was still alive beneath Alex's touch. There was no guilt. Or remorse. She still loved her husband, but what she felt for Alex was great. Different, but wonderful all the same.

Lisa was pleased Lilly was still asleep. It wasn't often she slept in, but this morning it was welcome. She wanted to spend some time with Alex alone before they were interrupted. Talk to him, kiss him, taste him. Reassure herself.

She scanned the living room and the kitchen but there was no sign of him. He must be outside already. She hugged the blanket tighter around her and tried to dull down her smile. Just because she was happy it didn't mean she had to go around grinning like a cat who'd caught a rabbit.

Lisa pushed open the door and stepped onto the porch. Her eyes hit his. She could tell he was watching, waiting for her. So why hadn't he just waited for her in bed?

He looked every part the soldier this morning. His eyes were steady, chin tilted, stance at ease. So different from William. More serious, more like a soldier even when he was off duty.

She noticed the change in his face, though. Recognized it from the man who'd arrived here, not the man she'd been with last night.

It worried her.

She could tell before he spoke that something was wrong. That something had changed from when she'd said good-night to him. What had happened between now and then?

"Alex, what are you doing out here?" she asked.

She slipped into a pair of flip-flops that were resting on the porch and walked the three steps down to the lawn. A touch of wet hit her toes—the ground was still damp from the night—but she barely felt it.

"Alex?"

"I haven't told you the truth." His voice was filled with grit.

She reached for his arm but he stayed still. Too still. She let her hand drop. He was pulling away from her. Emotionally, she knew that she'd lost him. That wall had gone up again. Even more so than before, if that were possible.

"There was a reason I came home and William didn't. You asked me if I saw how he died, and the answer is yes."

She wasn't sure where he was going with this, but she stayed silent. He'd already said yes when she'd asked him that question before, but there was obviously more to the story. Alex looked angry, and she didn't want to interrupt him.

"We were on a mission when he died. We'd finished. Thought it was over. But it wasn't."

She kept her eyes on his. He was hurting and all she could do was listen. His jaw was clenched so tight a stranger might guess it was wired so. A vein she'd never seen before strung a line down his neck.

"I was out in the open. William saw the enemy before I did. He called my name, distracted me, then threw himself over me." He walked backward a step but didn't break his stare. "I was meant to die that day, Lisa. They were aiming for me. He didn't have to do it—save me—but he did."

She didn't know what to say. It didn't make any difference. Not now. It didn't matter what he said. Her hands started to shake.

"He had everything to live for, Lisa. And I had nothing. It should have been me who died that day, me who came home in a body bag. Not him."

His eyes were tortured, flashing. His hurt stabbed her in the chest but she didn't let him see it. Kept it hidden, tucked away, not wanting him to see her emotion.

"If it wasn't for me your husband would still be coming

home. He'd still be alive," he reiterated, as though torturing himself with that truth.

"Alex." His name came out strangled, broken. "Alex, please…"

"Don't you see, Lisa? It's all my fault. Everything that's happened to you, what's happened to Lilly, it's *my* fault."

He punched out the words with such fury she didn't know what to do.

His words stung—not because they hurt her, but because they were so raw. Emotion cut through his body, his face, visible for all to see. Every angle, every plane of him was angry. Hurting.

A sob choked in her chest.

She had woken up this morning thinking it was the start of something fresh. That she and Alex had something special between them. Now he was ranting at her like he'd deliberately taken something precious from her, like he'd done something unforgivable. When all he'd done was be a soldier at war. A man. He'd done nothing wrong. How could he not see that?

"If you'd known this you never would have let me stay. You never would have invited me into your home."

He spat the words out and she didn't want to answer him—not when he was like this.

"If William hadn't been such a hero and I hadn't been so careless he'd be here right now. Not me."

And with that Alex spun around and started to march off.

"Don't you *dare*, Alex. You *cannot* walk away!" Her voice was tearful, but she fought to keep it strong.

He turned, his eyes wild, almost glaring at her. "Damn it, Lisa! I've wanted a family all my life. Dreamed about being brave enough to recreate what I lost as a boy."

She stared at him. Unblinking. Questions in her eyes.

"And you—you and Lilly—you've shown me that it's worth fighting for. That family does mean everything."

She nodded mutely.

"I'm sorry that I ruined your family. I am, Lisa. That's two families I've mucked up now."

"No, Alex." She glared back at him, incensed at what he was saying. "You were a boy when your parents died. A *boy*. You had nothing to do with it."

"If I hadn't asked them for an ice cream—if I hadn't begged them to take me for one—they'd still be alive. If William hadn't—"

Lisa reached for him, and this time he didn't fight her. He let himself be pulled into her arms. She held him like she would comfort a child.

"You know William would have done the same for any of his men. You *know* that, right?"

He stayed ominously still.

"You can't keep blaming yourself, Alex. You're an intelligent man. You know a child cannot take responsibility for death. For fate. Lilly wanted to go for a picnic the other day, but it wasn't her fault that we came across a bear."

Alex pulled back and watched her. She saw recognition in his eyes, but he still looked angry.

"Alex?"

He took a deep, shuddering breath.

"I understand, Alex." She kept hold of his arms. "It doesn't mean you stop hurting. It just means you need to let go of the blame you feel. The guilt. Don't let your past stop you from…"

He watched her intently.

"From a second-chance family."

He looked at her long and hard. Then he carefully detached her hands from his arms and turned around.

He started walking.

And he didn't look back.

Lisa's eyes were too filled with tears to watch where he went.

She fell down onto the porch step. Her legs folded, buckled and refused to hold her up. Her hands shook like they had received an electric current that had torn every thread of her skin. Her muscles felt weak, bones liquid.

She had gone through every emotion possible when William had died, when the messengers in uniform had knocked on her door to tell her the news in person. They'd asked her if she had someone to come and be with her, watched with doom-filled eyes as she'd dialed her sister with a shaking hand and asked her to come over.

When they'd told her, as Anna held her hand, she'd sobbed with the uselessness of the situation, knowing that he'd been dead how long—maybe hours? An entire day?—and she'd just gone about her business with no idea that her husband had been gunned down. Then she'd been angry, beaten at the sofa with all her might.

Then she'd felt relief. A sickening wash of relief that there would be no more days of worrying, of hoping he was okay. Because he'd already gone.

Up until the day Alex had arrived she had still been heaving with different emotions, feelings. She still was.

But this? This was equally bad.

Because she'd finally pushed through her sadness, her grief and her anger, and she'd been ready to start over again. Comfortable with the choice she'd made last night.

How wrong she'd been.

And now Alex was going to leave for good. She could feel it.

He was going to leave and she'd never see him again.

The man she had been slowly falling in love with was going to leave her, and there was nothing she could do about it.

A few months ago she'd felt like the black widow. As if life was over and she'd never be able to claw her way back to normality. Well, she had. She'd forced her head above water, gotten on with life despite her pain, and then found Alex on her doorstep.

The man had been a stranger to her then, but now he was real. And she wanted him to be there beside her as she started this life. She'd chosen to love Alex without guilt in her heart. But instead of returning that love he was going. Blaming himself for something he had never had the power to control. Holding on to pain from the past that she wanted to help him say goodbye to.

She loved him. If she hadn't loved him she never would have invited him into her bed last night.

Alex walked. He walked like he'd never walked before. As if there was a demon after him that wanted his life and if he stopped it would grab him by the throat.

He'd grabbed his pack from the car on the way past and it thumped rhythmically against his back now as he moved. What he needed was a night out in the open to clear his head. He couldn't care less if it was illegal to camp in the National Park. The place bordered the property, and it was surrounded by thousands of miles of forest. No one was going to bother about a single man minding his own business.

His feet pounded, ignoring the tug of roots as they tripped at his boots. The aroma of pine trees that he usually found so alluring did little to appease him. To tease the thunderous mood from him.

He'd told her the truth. The whole truth. He'd never forgive himself for what had happened that day, for not being alert enough to notice the snipers, for not screaming *no* at William as he'd moved to save him. For not acting fast enough himself and preventing the situation in the first place. Just like he'd never forgive himself for asking for ice cream that day of the crash. For putting his parents in the car that day.

Alex stopped. He stopped walking and braced one hand against a tree trunk to steady his breathing. And his mind.

It had all happened so fast. Too fast for him to do anything about it. Too fast for him to realize what was going on around him. Too fast for him to stop William from sacrificing his own life. Just like he'd been powerless as a boy.

His mind flashed to Lisa. To the torment on her face. He'd hurt her.

He should have told her right at the start. Should have explained what had happened and asked for her forgiveness that first day as they'd sat on the porch. Instead of letting things get this far before admitting his guilt. Instead of taking her to bed and letting her become intimate with the man she should be blaming for the way her life had turned out.

If he could take it back he would. If he could go back in time and take the bullets that had been destined for him he wouldn't hesitate. Not when it meant giving a woman her husband back and a child her father.

Because who would miss *him*? Who would even care that he was gone? Wasn't that why he had joined the army? Why he had always been so good at his job? Because he'd had no fear.

All his adult life he'd never had anything to live for, and it had made him fearless in the field.

Until now.

He had done his time in the army and he was finally putting that chapter of his life away. He'd never thought the day would come, but after William had died something inside him had had enough. He'd finished his tour and then asked to be relieved of his duty.

He might not have any plans, no idea of what he wanted to do yet, but it didn't involve the army. Not anymore.

The only thing he *was* sure about was that he couldn't stay here. Not now. He had to leave.

Lisa would probably have his stuff packed. She'd probably already chucked his belongings in the back of his car and was waiting to bid him farewell.

A knife stabbed at the muscles of his stomach, but he ignored it as he would a hunger pang.

Then he started marching.

The demon was after him again and he wanted to lose it.

* * *

He'd crossed the spot she'd mentioned that time they'd all been out together. Close to the neighbor's boundary. Then he'd followed the river until he'd come to a trail, and then he'd walked until he was exhausted.

He should have brought his rod with him. A man could only walk so far. Even he knew that. And yet his anger, his determination and guilt, had seen him pound out miles even he hadn't known he was capable of.

If he'd brought a line with him at least he could have eaten.

Alex guessed it to be about two o'clock. He squinted up at the sun. Yes, at least two. He fell in a messy heap to the ground and dragged his pack off his back.

He'd thrown the bag together before he'd left the mainland, thinking he'd be camping his first night out, but it still didn't hold everything he needed.

There was a box of wax matches, a few snack bars, his sleeping bag, and a tall bottle of water. He pulled off the lid and sculled a few deep mouthfuls.

It was stupid, his being out here without preparing properly first, but it wasn't as if his decision to march off into a national park had been made via logical conclusions.

He knew how to survive, could fend for himself for a decent amount of time out here if he had to, but he didn't really fancy being this far from civilization. Not at this time of year, when the bears were still hungry. Not to mention the wolves he'd heard call out in the night from the cabin.

He jumped back to his feet. What he needed was enough wood to start a fire. At least that would keep predators and any four-legged foes at bay.

Alex started to work. He scouted the site for timber, and his search didn't take him far. But he still worked up a sweat. Wet heat clung to his forehead and neck. He removed his shirt and wiped his skin, before tucking it into the back of his jeans. Then he sought out stones for the fire's perimeter, which proved harder. He marked his trail, lightly, and headed back out to the river-edge. It took him at least half an hour to walk in and out with the first load of stones, but the next two trips were shorter.

By now he'd only counted one sign of wildlife. Two elk drinking greedily from the river. They'd scarpered fast when they'd seen him.

The loud twitter of birds had built to an almost deafening crescendo. He was pleased they were only just starting to sing like that. It meant he still had time to get this fire belting out heat and a steady flame glowing before darkness fell like a consuming blanket.

He pushed away the thoughts that niggled at his mind. He might have been stupid coming, but he was here now, and if anything he could punish himself by sleeping rough for the night.

He tinkered with the fire, blowing on the dried leaves he'd built up in the centre, cupping his hands to stop the wind dispelling the lick of flame that tickled the base of the leaves.

It only took him one try to get the fire breathing back at him.

Alex reached for a second snack bar and chewed each mouthful slowly. It had to last him until morning.

He had a feeling he should rest now too. When the wolves started their nightly ritual and sang to the forest, or the rustle of animal moved between the trees, he wasn't going to get any shut-eye. Plus he wanted to keep that fire stoked all night, to make sure he didn't become part of the food chain.

Alex took the waterproof sheet from his pack and strung it between the low branches of three trees that surrounded his spot. It was close enough to the fire to allow protection and a glimmer of heat, and the way the trees met with thick brush meant his back would be partly protected.

He dragged his T-shirt back over his head as the air began to cool around him, threw another few branches on the fire and slipped into his sleeping bag.

On second thought... He unzipped the end so his feet poked

out. At least he'd be able to run quickly if something did happen. The idea of being stuck helpless inside a bag was not one he wanted to entertain.

It was dark, and still he hadn't come home. Lisa was starting to worry.

The trouble was, she didn't want to call her mother or her sister. What would she tell them? That the man she'd kept insisting was just a visitor had left, as he was entitled to, and not returned? It wasn't like she was wanting to keep tabs on him, but walking out into the forest and not coming back before dark was not something she had expected him to do. Even that angry, she hadn't expected him to do that.

Alex never would have left the rental car sitting in her drive if he wasn't coming back, and his things were still in the cabin. She didn't have to check to know that.

Right now all she cared about was seeing his large frame walk back up her lawn. Seeing his shadow move behind the blind in the cabin. Or hearing his knock at the door.

She'd locked it, for safety, but she was ready to open it if he arrived home.

Home. It was a word she knew well. But she knew the same could not be said for him. It hurt her knowing that he had no one and nowhere to call on.

This was a man who had turned up on her doorstep looking for her. A man who had seemed so traumatized that there was no hope for him. But she'd seen a transformation firsthand. Seen the change in him when Lilly started to talk to him. Felt the change in him when they were together, just like she'd felt it within herself.

As Lilly had found her words, so Alex had seemed to start finding himself. Whoever that might be. She liked him whatever way he came, because she knew that deep down he was a kind, brave, honest person. He was just hurting. And she wanted to help him.

Her heart continued its steady thump against the wall of her chest. She tried to swallow but her mouth kept drying out.

She went to check on Lilly again. Her little girl was snoring, ever so lightly. Boston raised his head, then tucked back into her.

Before William's passing Boston hadn't been allowed on the bed. Now he slept with Lilly every night. If it brought her daughter comfort she was happy to turn a blind eye to the hair he left behind.

Lisa walked to the window one last time. She pressed her forehead against the glass and conjured an image of him. Of Alex.

He was a soldier, she reminded herself. That meant he could survive.

And when was the last time a human had been taken by a bear in these parts? Plenty of people camped in the National Park.

She quickly rid her mind of thoughts of camping. The average tourist stuck to the camping grounds. They didn't just take off and set up camp wherever their feet stopped walking.

Lisa pulled her eyes away. It was so dark out she couldn't see a thing anyway. The lights on her porch didn't filter light out that far.

She went downstairs and pulled her wheat bag from the bottom drawer. She put it in the microwave to heat it.

Lisa watched as the numbers counted down from four minutes. That was as long as she'd give herself. Four full minutes until the bag was hot, then she was turning in for the night.

There was nothing she could do to help Alex except try and make him see reason when he eventually turned up again.

She was no use traipsing off into the forest with a torch. She couldn't even call the local park ranger. Their trainee had left a few months back, and the ranger who had served the area for two decades had suffered a heart attack. Right now it was just a group of townsmen who'd banded together to take turns until a replacement was found.

Her brother-in-law was one of those men. She wasn't going to wake her sister up at this time of the night.

All she could do was wait it out.

William. She called him in her mind. He would never have done anything silly like this—walking off into the forest and staying out after dark. But then William hadn't been troubled like Alex. William had been a talker. Had grown up with love and without pain.

She liked that both men were so different. It helped her to know she wasn't trying to replicate what she'd had with William.

Alex had shown her she did want to love again.

If only he'd come back and give her the chance to tell him that.

CHAPTER TWELVE

THE door to the cottage was open. Alex fought against the clench of his jaw and forced his feet up the steps. His entire being felt shattered. Exhausted. More emotionally wrung out than he'd ever been.

His back ached, his mind was drained, and all he wanted to do was have a hot shower and rid himself of any memory of the hours he'd walked or the night he'd spent sleeping rough.

He had expected a mess. He had wondered if Lisa would throw all his things in a heap or politely have them waiting for him in the car. Thought she would have become angry, furious with him for what he'd done.

He was wrong on both counts.

Lilly was sitting on his bed. So was Boston. He ignored the dirty paw marks and levelled his eyes at Lilly instead. "Hi."

She gazed up at him. He could see questions in her eyes, things she wanted to ask, but he didn't push her. He didn't want to. He didn't even think he wanted to know what the questions were.

"Alex," she answered.

He hadn't got off as easily as he'd hoped. His head ached—an insistent, dull drumming of pain that banged at his forehead. He dropped to the seat across from the bed and looked at the little girl.

The last thing he'd wanted was to get close to her. In some ways he still felt nervous about how to talk to her, what to say, what to do around her. But other times it just seemed so natural to hang out with her and help her through her not speaking. Like they were connected by what had happened. But when he looked in her eyes he still saw what she'd lost. And it hurt.

"Alex, I know you're not my daddy, but sometimes I wish you were," she said in a small voice.

His eyes snapped shut. No. No, no, *no*. This was why he couldn't be here. Shouldn't be here.

He *wasn't* her father. He could never fill that role. And here she was, saying words that she didn't understand. Not knowing what had happened over there. Why her father had died and under what circumstances.

"Lilly…" He could barely whisper her name.

"I think Boston would like you as his dad too," she continued.

Alex crushed the fingers of his left hand with his right, and tried to control the tic in his cheek and the pounding of his heart. It felt like his pulse was about to rupture from his skin.

She jumped from the bed with Boston in pursuit. "Want to come fishing?"

Alex shook his head. "Not right now, Lilly."

She shrugged and ran off.

He tried to put his mind back together, like a tricky puzzle missing some of its pieces.

A knife had just been turned in his heart, giving him a fatal blow, so how was it he was still breathing? Why was it that the idea of being a daddy to that little girl had fired something within him that he hadn't even known existed?

He heard laughter, and then muffled talking from outside. Alex rose to close the door, then lay back on the bed.

He had no idea what to do.

He'd fought getting too close to anyone, being part of a family for so long. Now he felt as though he was on a precipice, dangerously close to the edge. One wrong move and he was lost.

* * *

"Alex?" Lisa tapped at the door. Her knuckles fell softly against the timber as she called.

A noise made her step back. She didn't want to be too in his face—not after how he'd acted last night. Not when she didn't know what was happening inside his mind.

But at the same time she wanted to scream. To yell at him and tell him how worried she had been, how she'd lain awake all night and prayed that he'd survive the night and then come back to her.

The door swung open. Relief hit her in the gut and stole the breath from her lungs, left her throat dry.

He looked terrible. Like a man who'd been out on the town for nights on end. Only she knew he hadn't. The darkness under his eyes was from the never-ending cycle of guilt and anger that she was determined to dispel. Even if she hated that he'd walked away, wanted to shake him and curse at him, she still wanted to throw her arms around him and hold him tight and beg him never to leave her like that ever again.

No matter what happened between them she wanted to help him. And there was one way she could do that. Without telling him anything, without letting her emotions take hold and make her say or do something she could regret, what she needed to do was *show* him something.

"Alex, I wondered if you might come somewhere with me?"

He looked wary. She understood. He'd expected her to be angry with him, to blame him, to shout back at him, but she didn't. She'd known William too well for that. If he'd decided to put himself in the line of fire to save another man—well, that had been his choice and she admired him for it. When it was your time to go, it was your time. Alex had had nothing to do with that. Just like as a boy he'd played no part in his parents' death.

She also didn't want him to know that she'd noticed his absence while he'd spent the night camping. Noticed it as if one of her vital organs had been slipped from her body for an entire night.

He just stood, watching her still, his eyes unfocused yet looking at her.

"Please?" she said.

He shifted his weight, then went back inside. She waited. He emerged maybe four minutes later with his boots on, hair damp from the quick shower he'd managed.

"Where are we going?" Even his voice sounded husky, like he was hungover.

She smiled at him. "You'll see. Go get in the truck and I'll grab Lilly."

He waited. He let his forehead rest against the butt of his hand as he leaned on the door. It was as if all his energy had drained through his feet and left them heavy with the residue of it.

He saw movement and looked up. Lilly was holding her mother's hand as they crossed down and over to the car. She jumped up beside him and sat in the middle of the bench seat before Lisa jumped behind the wheel.

"No Boston today?" he asked, trying to make normal conversation.

Lisa shook her head. "He'll be fine here for a little while. We're not going to be that long."

He looked back out the window. He had no idea where they were going and he didn't much care. When they got back he was going to leave. He couldn't stay.

They rumbled along the road in silence. Even Lilly stayed quiet.

Alex sat there and observed. That was all he could do. There was nothing he could say, nothing he wanted to say, and Lisa had turned up the radio—presumably in an effort to avoid conversation.

They pulled up outside a nice enough single-level home. It

was set back off the road and sported a rustic feel, like most of the places they'd passed on their way here.

"We'll just be a minute," Lisa said.

Lilly reached out and skimmed her fingers against his, before smiling at him and following her mom out the door.

A lump formed in his throat but he pushed it away. He didn't want to watch them but he had to. Couldn't drag his eyes away if he tried.

He saw Lisa's sister emerge from the house. They embraced and Lisa kissed her cheek. Her sister placed her arm around Lilly and led her inside.

Lisa started to walk back to the car. He was pleased her sister hadn't acknowledged him—it was, after all, what he deserved—but then maybe she hadn't even seen him.

She got into the cab and started the engine. They pulled back out onto the road. He wanted to ask her where they were going but he didn't.

She could take him wherever she liked.

The silence in the car became knife-edged. Although she hadn't really needed confirmation to guess that he wouldn't like cemeteries.

Every time she came here she thought of the funeral service. Now she wished Alex had been there to say goodbye to William too. Maybe it would have helped him find closure.

The memory of the jolt that had run through her body when the guns were raised and fired in a final salute still hit her spine every time she visited, but it was less pronounced than it had been the day of the service.

Full military honors and nothing less, and it had been very fitting for her husband. She'd taken home the flag passed to her by his commanding officer and tucked it in a special box in Lilly's wardrobe, there for her to have when she was old enough to appreciate it. Along with his uniform.

She cut the engine and turned in her seat to face Alex.

"Come with me," she instructed.

Alex wouldn't look at her.

"Alex?"

"No." He threw the word at her.

"I need you to come with me," she said firmly. She opened her door and took a punt that he'd follow her. Eventually. She traced the path to William's headstone, standing white, tall and proud amongst many older ones.

Lisa came here every week. Every Sunday she usually came with Lilly, and they ran a rag over the stone to clean it and placed fresh flowers in the grate.

It didn't hurt her coming here—at least not the sharp pain it had been to start with. Now she just wanted to make William proud by looking after him, looking out for him even in death. To show him that she loved him still.

Lisa felt a presence behind her. She didn't turn to look. She knew Alex was there.

"William was a great man," she said, forcing her voice to cooperate. "But he had many different roles."

Alex stood still behind her. She could feel the size of him, the warmth of his body, as he stood his ground. This had to be uncomfortable for him, but she hoped he wouldn't walk away.

"William was a son, a husband, a father and a soldier. He valued each role, but his life was the life of a soldier, and we all knew and accepted that. *I* accepted that."

She studied the headstone and hoped William could hear them. He *had* been a good man. She wasn't just saying it because he wasn't around to defend himself. He'd been great at everything he'd turned his hand to, but the role he'd been most destined for had been that of a soldier. He'd been a patriot, had strongly believed in serving his country, and she had never, ever resented that. Even now that he was gone she wouldn't let herself feel that way. She'd loved that he believed in serving and protecting. Apart from missing him when he was away, he had been the husband she'd always dreamed of.

"William was a soldier because he believed in fighting for

what was right. He was the type of man who would jump into a lake to save another human even if it meant he could drown himself. And that's why he saved you that day, Alex. Because that's the type of man he was."

She turned then. Let her feet swivel until she was facing Alex.

He didn't look any better than he had earlier, but she knew he'd listened. He could look her in the eye now, and that was more than he'd been able to do earlier.

"What I'm trying to say," she said, slowly reaching her arms up until her hands rested on his shoulders, "is that he couldn't *not* have saved you. It wasn't your fault that he died. He would have saved whoever was in the line of fire, and that day it just happened to be you."

Alex looked like he was going to cry.

In all her years as a married woman she had never, ever seen a man cry. William had smiled, laughed, shown anger on the odd occasion. But not even when Lilly was born had he cried.

She pulled Alex into her arms and held him as tight as she could, as if he were Lilly and needed all the comfort in her mother's heart. Alex resisted for a heartbeat, before falling against her. Clinging to her.

He buried his face in her hair and held on to her. Hard.

"William wouldn't judge us, Alex. He wouldn't. If I thought I was disrespecting him I never would have let anything happen between us. I admit that it took me a while to feel that way, but I do honestly believe it now."

His hold didn't change. She had thought he might shed some tears, but he was holding them firmly in check. She almost wished he'd let it go. She knew that holding tears back did nothing to help. That to move on sometimes you had to let go.

Alex straightened and cleared his throat.

"I'm sorry you feel like William's death was your fault, Alex. I really am. But I don't blame you, and I never will. You need to stop blaming yourself too," she said.

She didn't wait for him to respond. Instead she turned around, closed her eyes, and whispered a silent prayer. It was the same one she said every time.

Alex still stood behind her. He hadn't moved.

"I'm going to go back to the truck now," she told him.

He nodded. "Give me a minute, okay?"

She walked one step toward him, stretched to whisper a kiss on his cheek, then left him.

This was what she'd hoped for. That she could bring him here, tell it like it was, and leave him alone to make peace with William.

She got in the car and watched him.

Alex had crouched down. His long legs buckled under him as he squatted in front of the headstone, reading the words, then he sat back on the grass.

Lisa wanted to look away, to give him privacy, but she also wanted the chance to watch him while he couldn't see her.

The night before last had been incredible. Even if he had woken up troubled about what they'd done it had been amazing. Being in Alex's arms, being caught up against his skin, had been more than she'd ever experienced. Made her realize how different he was from William and how much she appreciated that.

His touch had filled every vein within her body with fiery light, made her want to keep him in her bed and never let him out. But it had been more than just physical. For the second time in her life she had fallen in love. Truly fallen in love.

She almost felt guilty. How was it that she'd had the privilege to fall in love twice? To have two amazing men come into her life and be able to love them both? She felt incredibly lucky, so special. She'd thought it would feel wrong, that it would trouble her, but it didn't at all.

Alex fought the urge to sink to his knees. He wished the ground would open up and swallow him in William's place, but he pushed the thought away.

He needed this. He needed this so badly—to say goodbye and ask William for forgiveness.

While they had been friends in real life, after leaving the army their paths might never have crossed again. Yet now their lives had intertwined in a way that neither of them could ever have imagined.

I'm sorry, William. He closed his eyes and reached one hand out to the tombstone, the cold hitting his palm. *I wish I could make things different, but I think I've fallen for your wife.*

Alex's heart twisted at the silent confession. He still didn't want to admit it, but whenever he thought of Lisa, whenever he acknowledged what had happened between them, he knew something inside of him had changed irrevocably.

And it terrified him.

But William had loved his wife. And he'd also valued their friendship and what they'd shared throughout the years.

Deep down Alex knew what William would say in response to his confession. He'd heard the words himself as he'd listened to him gasp his final breath.

Tell Lisa I want her to be happy.

Alex knew he'd meant it, had seen it in the openness of his friend's eyes despite the pain.

If Alex truly believed he could make Lisa and Lilly happy, then William would give him his blessing.

He sighed and dropped into a crouch, sitting low to the earth once more.

Goodbye, my friend.

Alex caught Lisa's eye as he stretched to his feet.

She met his eyes through the windscreen and saw what she'd hoped to see. He smiled at her.

A tickle traced her skin like a feather. Had she finally managed to put a sledgehammer through that wall? That fierce, impenetrable depth of solid concrete that had kept his heart tucked away?

The dread that had traipsed through her like a spiky stiletto was replaced with a nerve-edged flutter of calm.

Maybe they did have a chance. Just maybe they did.

The cottage was almost finished, and the thought of him leaving early made her want to convulse in pain. Maybe getting through to him like this would make him hang around longer. Every pore in her skin longed for him to stay.

CHAPTER THIRTEEN

"COME in with me to get Lilly."

Alex didn't particularly want to go in to Anna's house, but he did.

They walked up to the front door together, side by side.

"Anna's husband is called Sam. You'll like him," she promised.

"Was he a friend of William's?" Alex asked dryly.

"His best friend."

Alex stopped. He couldn't help it.

Lisa grabbed him by the arm and tugged him. Firmly. "Come on. You've got that look about you that you had that first day on my porch. Sam's not going to bite, and neither is Anna."

He let himself be led.

He wasn't so sure she was right about her sister, though.

But Lisa had been there for him today when he'd needed her. When all he'd wanted was to run, to be alone, she had guided him from the darkness into the light.

For the first time since his parents' death he had finally let someone in.

The house was exactly as he'd expected. The hallway was slightly dim, but it led into a large living room that was filled with Alaskan sun.

"Yoo-hoo! Hello?"

No one had answered when Lisa had knocked at the front door, so they had just walked on in.

He saw Lilly first. She was sitting outside in the sun with her aunt, painting. They had a huge sheet of something, and Lilly had a paintbrush in one hand and a tube in the other.

A man he guessed was Sam sat slightly in the shade, with a bottle of beer resting on his knee.

"Want a drink?"

Alex looked over at Lisa. She had the door to the fridge open.

"Sure."

"Beer?"

He nodded.

She popped the top on two bottles and passed him one. He took a long sip before following her outside.

He had a feeling he was going to need the infusion of alcohol to make it through this afternoon.

Earlier, he had thought Lisa would be on the verge of kicking him to the curb. Now he was at her sister's place. With her. As if they'd moved on and were taking a giant step forward together.

He took another swig. Lisa had bent down to talk to Lilly, and Sam was looking at him.

He smiled. Sam smiled back before rising to his feet.

It appeared not to be a hostile situation.

The air had a faint tinge of night to it. Lisa could smell the hint of rain leaving a dampness in the air before it even fell.

"We might have to relocate inside for dinner."

Lisa watched Alex as he helped gather up some plates with Sam. It had gone down pretty well, having him here with her, even if Anna *was* a touch on the sulky side.

"Lilly." She called her daughter over. "I think it's time to go wash your hands."

Lilly bolted into the house and headed for the washroom.

Alex walked beside Lisa, juggling plates. She took some

of the load. Their eyes met, flashed at one another before she looked away.

Lisa was pleased he was enjoying himself. There had been a tension between them that she hated, and she had wanted to dispel it as fast as possible. Last night, which he'd spent goodness only knew where, had been one of the most painful, the most worrisome of her life. She liked him, had fallen for him, and she didn't want to see him hurt, alone, so lost ever again. She also didn't want him to leave. Not yet. Not until they'd figured out what was happening between them.

Anna called out to her from the kitchen. She went to investigate as Alex joined Sam back outside.

Her sister was tossing a salad.

"Want me to take care of the potatoes?" Lisa asked.

Anna nodded in their direction. "Dish—top right-hand corner."

Lisa reached into the cupboard for it and gently brought it down.

"So, you guys are out of the closet now, huh?" Anna sniped.

Lisa put the bowl down. That type of question didn't warrant an answer.

"Come on, Lisa. I can see the way you look at one another."

Her face flushed hot. She wasn't embarrassed. It was just...

"Lisa?"

She spun around and waved a spoon with all the fury she could muster. "Enough, Anna—*enough*," she snapped. "We are *not* in a relationship, but if we decide to be it won't be based on whether or not we have *your* permission. I'm sick of trying to please everyone."

Anna glared at her. Her eyes were angry, wild. Lisa had hardly ever seen her sister looking like that. Not since they'd been kids and she'd broken the head off of her Barbie doll.

"It's too soon, Lisa. William's only been—"

"I said *enough*! Don't ruin a perfectly nice evening by sticking your nose where it shouldn't be," Lisa said.

Both their heads snapped up when a deep noise rang out.

Lisa felt guilty when she saw Alex standing there. He'd cleared his throat—loudly—to alert them, but how long had he been there? How much had he heard?

She glared at Anna. Her sister just shrugged. Lisa knew what it was about. Her sister wanted her to be miserable, to stay a widow and never emerge. Well, she wasn't going to, and no one was going to tell her when it was okay to come out of mourning. No one. She wasn't trying to replace her husband. Never! But she also wasn't about to be guilted into not moving on.

"Alex, could you help me carry this out?" Lisa asked.

"Sure." He jumped to attention.

She grabbed him before he reached her, stopped him with a hand to his chest, and stood on her tiptoes to plant a smacker of a kiss on his lips.

He didn't move. The stunned look on his face was priceless.

"Thanks," she said. "Here." She passed him the dish.

Alex walked out, still in a daze.

"You'll catch a fly if you keep your mouth open like that," Lisa commented to Anna.

Her sister clamped her mouth shut and stared at her in disbelief.

Lisa just shrugged. Two could play at this game. It wasn't her style, but she was sick and tired of being the serious one, of trying to please others.

Lilly adored Alex, and so did she. Right now that was all that mattered.

Alex still couldn't quite shake off the memory of that quick kiss. Even now, after dinner.

He sat with Sam while the girls nattered. He hadn't missed the tension between the sisters earlier, but they'd obviously pushed past it. Or they were just ignoring it for now and leaving the arguing until later. In private.

"Did you serve with William for long?"

Alex turned back to Sam. He had completely lost the focus of their conversation. He angled himself so he couldn't look at Lisa in order to give Sam his full attention.

Not that he particularly wanted to talk about William right now, but it would be rude not to reply.

He thought about the cemetery again, and calm passed over him. If Lisa could forgive him, then he owed it to himself to do the same.

For some reason hearing Lisa say William's name held less punch. Perhaps because she talked about him fondly, but with finality. Everyone else seemed to talk about him like he was still going to walk back in the door.

"We served together a few times, but this last time we were in the same unit permanently for around two months—maybe longer." He didn't say it, but it would have been much longer than that if they'd both served out the full tour.

Their friendship had been the kind that could only be formed by trusting another person so much it was as if they were a part of you. Knowing how they reacted, how they moved. He and William had been like that.

Sam nodded and held up another beer. Alex shook his head and motioned toward Lisa. "I think I'll drive. She's had a couple."

Sam opened one for himself and sat back. "William and I went way back. We both started dating the girls our last year of senior high."

Alex had guessed they'd been friends a long time.

"I can see why William liked you," Sam added.

"Yeah?"

Sam grinned at him. "Lisa obviously doesn't mind you either."

Alex felt uncomfortable. Was he joking for real, trying to hint at something, or saying it was okay?

"Sam, I—"

The other guy held up the hand that gripped his beer. "What you and Lisa do is your own business. I'm not part of the gossip brigade."

"Your wife sure doesn't seem happy about it," Alex pointed out.

He watched as Sam smiled over at his wife. Lisa looked their way too. It was as if the girls knew they were being talked about.

"Lisa's her little sister. Anna's just looking out for her."

"What about the rest of Brownswood?" Alex said ruefully.

Sam shrugged. "Small-town life is what it is. It's whether you care about the talk that matters." He looked hard at Alex. "And I don't take you for the type to care what strangers think."

"Guess you're right."

His attention was back on Lisa. She had risen, and was rubbing at her arms like she was cold. He ached to go to her and warm her, put his arms around her, but he didn't want to do anything that might upset her sister. Not if it would upset Lisa too. He didn't know if she would be okay with it.

He had expected tonight, this afternoon, to be dreadful. Expected to be judged, to find Sam hostile, but it had been half good. Better than good. It had been nice to have a beer with another guy—one who didn't want to interrogate him about war—and just behave like a regular citizen.

But then if the guy had been one of William's best buddies he probably knew enough about war to have already satisfied any curiosity he might have had.

It just felt good to feel normal. Something he hadn't felt in a long time.

Alex drove home. Lisa and Lilly were tucked up close to one another across from him, and he navigated through the steady path of rain that was falling on the road. He was pleased he'd refused a third beer. The road was slippery and he wouldn't have liked Lisa to be driving.

"You were right about the rain."

Lisa just smiled.

"Your sister was—"

"Wrong." She cut him off. "My sister was wrong."

He smiled. Was she just being stubborn because she didn't like her sister telling her what to do?

"We don't often argue, but tonight she was most definitely wrong."

"Who was wrong, Mommy?" Lilly asked sleepily.

Alex shook his head at Lisa. He wasn't going to tell if she wasn't.

"No one, honey. Alex and I are just being silly."

He pulled up outside the house and scooped Lilly up to ferry her inside. The rain was coming down hard now, trickling down his neck and wetting his hair. He managed to keep Lilly mostly dry.

Whining echoed on the other side of the door and Lilly called out. "Boston! We're home!"

Lisa emerged next to them. Wet.

She thrust the key into the lock and turned the handle. Lilly disappeared with her dog.

"To bed, young lady!" Lisa called after her. Then she turned to face Alex, pulling the door shut behind her.

The look on her face was...open.

"Do you mind telling me what that stunt in the kitchen was about?" he asked.

She grinned. "Proving to my sister that she was wrong."

"And that's all it was?" he wanted to know.

Her eyes glinted at him. "Maybe."

He shuffled forward so he was only a foot away from her. He absorbed the sight of her wet hair, just damp enough to cling to her head, the lashes that were coated with a light sting of rain. Then his eyes dropped to her lips.

She parted them. Her eyes lifted to look into his.

"We have everything stacked against us, Lisa. Everything," he warned. Then he bent slightly, so their lips could touch. Just.

Lisa let her body fall against his.

"Not everything, Alex." She sighed into his mouth as she said the words.

He tried to pull back, but couldn't. She rubbed her lips over his, teasing him, pulling him in deeper than he had intended going.

"I just don't want you to feel guilty about this later. About *me*," he insisted.

She disagreed. "We are both grown, consenting adults."

"It's not enough," he argued. He wanted to resist. He really, badly, desperately wanted to resist. But this was Lisa. This was the woman who had already forgiven him his sins and still wanted him.

It was Lisa who pulled back this time. "It's enough because there is no one judging us—no one that matters." She looked up at him. "Lilly is the most important thing in my life, and she accepts you. William would have accepted you. And in my heart I know we're not doing anything wrong."

He nodded. He knew it was the truth, but he had needed to hear it from her.

"And your family?" he asked.

"My family only want to protect me. Don't want to see me hurt. It's not that they don't like you," she insisted.

They looked at one another.

"You're not going to leave, are you, Alex? Not yet?"

He shook his head. "No."

"You're not just staying because of Lilly, though, are you? You don't have to worry about hurting my feelings, and I can comfort her—honestly. You shouldn't feel like you're trapped here," she said.

What? He traced a tender finger from the edge of her mouth down to the top of her collarbone. *Never.*

"I'm not just staying because of Lilly," he said gruffly.

"But…"

He shook his head. He felt the sadness of his smile and forced it to lift. "I shouldn't be here at all, Lisa. But I'm here because of you."

She leaned heavily against him. He felt her relief.

His mind started to play tricks on him again. A cloud of doubt hovered over his brain. "Do you only want me here because of Lilly? Because I helped her?"

She shook her head. Vigorously. "No."

Relief emptied his clouds of worry.

"I trust you, so trust me," he said.

"We're going to the Kennedys' place for dinner tomorrow night," she mumbled into his chest, not looking at him.

He gulped. Please, no… That was too much.

She looked back up at him and gave him the sweetest of smiles.

"Time for bed, Alex." She gave him a brief kiss on the lips—nothing like before.

He still stood there, stunned at hearing they were going to William's parents' house.

"Do it for me, Alex. It's just dinner."

He kept his eyes on her as she swept inside and closed the door on him. He heard the lock twist. She was punishing him still, he realized. She'd forgiven him—she'd shown him that today—but was still punishing him for running out on her after making love to her, and then spending the night in the forest by himself.

He was just coming to terms with what he'd done, and now he had to face William's parents. Great. His boots felt like they were filled with the heaviest of cement. Eating a meal with the parents of the man who'd died saving him wasn't exactly his idea of fun. But if he was going to try to move on, to open himself up, then maybe it was something he had to do.

The cottage loomed in front of him. He wished he was up in Lisa's bed with her, instead of trudging in the rain to the cabin.

Lying there in her bed, stretched out on her soft sheets, waiting for her to join him.

But he wasn't going there. Not yet anyway. He needed time to think.

Especially about tomorrow night's dinner.

Besides, Lisa had already locked the door on him.

Seeing William's gravestone today had helped him. But seeing William's parents and answering any questions they might have? Well, that was something else entirely.

He hoped he was up for it.

CHAPTER FOURTEEN

"I UNDERSTAND your loss."

He watched the looks cross George and Sally's faces and knew what they were thinking. It was what he'd thought every time someone had said those words to him.

"My parents died when I was eleven years old. We were driving home from an ice cream parlour and a car went through an intersection. They were killed instantly," he told them.

He didn't look at Lisa while he said it. Couldn't.

Almost worse than the sadness of losing his parents had been the pity. That was why he usually kept it to himself. But somehow tonight, sitting with these people, he needed to say it.

Alex looked at William's parents. He didn't see pity there. Instead he saw understanding.

Lisa reached for his hand beneath the table. He was relieved to feel her touch, but he knew he was strong enough to continue. He knew Lisa accepted him for who he was, understood that now, but being here meant a lot to him. It was the final missing piece of the puzzle to allow him to move on and stop looking back to his past.

"Do you have any other family?"

He shook his head at Sally's question.

"I went into foster care, then I joined the army as soon as I was of age."

* * *

Lisa couldn't believe he'd opened up like that.

The connection he had with Lilly was very real, and hearing his story, the full version of it, made her realize why.

Alex knew pain and loss more than anyone.

All of her own life she had felt so loved, so nurtured. As a married woman she had again known love, of a different kind, and then with Lilly she'd known she'd never be alone again.

But Alex—he was trying to start over, to put past demons behind him, and she wanted so badly to be there for him.

Lilly burst into the room then. The smile lighting her face was infectious.

"Hello, darling." Sally smiled at her granddaughter.

Lisa held her breath. The expression on her daughter's face had taken her by surprise.

Lilly looked at Alex. He moved his head, only just, but Lisa didn't miss it. Lilly smiled up at him.

"May I have dessert, Grandma?"

Lisa suppressed a squeal of delight. Sally had tears in her eyes, but—bless her soul—she just got up as if nothing was out of the ordinary.

"How does ice cream with chocolate sauce sound?" Sally asked.

Lilly giggled and sidled up to her, before winking at Alex.

Sally stopped as she passed Alex and let her hand rest on his shoulder. "Thank you, Alex. You've done her the world of good."

Alex smiled back.

He had brought light back into their lives like only William had done in the past. He had filled Lisa's world with hope for the future, had helped Lilly to find her voice again, and brought comfort to William's parents. Sharing stories. Telling them how highly their son had been respected by his men.

"Lisa, do you mind if I steal Alex away for a single malt Scotch?" George asked.

She emerged from her daydream and nodded. William had

always joined his father for a Scotch after dinner, so it was nice that Alex could share in that for one night.

"I'll join the girls in the kitchen," she said.

She rounded the corner and found her mother-in-law and daughter curled in front of the fire in the lounge. She stopped to listen to them talk.

It was like Lilly had never lost her voice.

The therapist had said this might happen. That one day she could just start talking again to everyone around her.

She'd seen the look Alex had given her daughter, though. Seen Lilly looking to him for guidance. Whatever he'd said, whatever they'd talked about earlier, it had obviously worked.

There was nothing about this situation that seemed entirely comfortable to Alex.

He didn't think he'd ever pass the buck on the guilt that still kept him awake at night sometimes, but at least this family had found comfort in his being here.

"Son, it doesn't take a genius to figure out you're troubled," George said.

Alex took the just-warm Scotch thrown over a handful of ice. He raised his glass, a brief advance in the air, as George did the same. It tore a fiery path down his throat that didn't disappear until it reached his stomach.

"Lisa and Lilly are the only family we have," the other man went on.

Alex understood how protective George must feel over them, but he'd made peace with Lisa, been accepted, and that was what he had to hold true to.

"I'm sorry that I couldn't help bring your son back alive. As God is my witness, I'd have traded places with him in an instant. But if Lisa wants me here I'm not going to turn my back on her," he said.

George sat back in his chair. "I'm not here to lecture you, Alex. You've brought happiness with you that some of us thought was lost forever. I want to thank you."

Alex sipped at his drink. He didn't know what to say.

"If you want to be in Lisa's life, in Lilly's life, we say welcome to the family."

Alex's palm was filled with George's. With the hand of William's father. He'd thought it would seem wrong, would fly in the face of the guilt that had tormented him these past few months, but it didn't.

Warmth spread through his fingers, and it didn't stop there. It traveled up his arm. Shook his shoulders. Hit him in the head.

For the first time since the night his parents had died Alex felt a burning ball form in his throat. Tears bristled behind his eyes.

He couldn't have answered if he'd wanted to.

Not without letting another grown man see him cry.

"I'd like to hear some stories when you're ready. Hear more about William. About what you went through over there."

Alex jumped to his feet, glass snatched firmly between his fingers. He swallowed the lump and turned his head at an angle.

He couldn't see anything out the window except blackness. Nothingness. It suited him just fine.

Tears stung his skin as they hit. He sniffed. Hard. Then wiped at his face. He swilled the last of his Scotch, then slung it back.

It burnt, but not as badly as his tears.

Alex wiped at his face once more and forced them back.

He felt lighter. The guilt that had sucked him dry was now turning to liquid and hydrating him once more. He was powerless to stop feeling as if everything had been lifted from his chest, the pressure finally gone.

"William took a bullet for me, George. I'll forever be grateful for that."

Alex closed his eyes as memories played back through his mind. For the first time in a long while he wanted to talk about the friend he'd lost. About how much those wartime friendships had meant to him, and how he'd never give up those memories even if he could. It was time.

Lisa pulled the covers tight up to her chin and tried to shut her mind off.

Tonight had gone better than she'd thought it would. Much better.

Sally and George's blessing meant a lot to her, but it went deeper than that. The change in Lilly was extraordinary. Exciting. But it worried her. The therapist's words kept echoing in her head. What if Alex *did* leave and she became worse than before? The thought sent a crawl of dread through her body. They'd only agreed on a few weeks. But now he had said he'd stay longer.

Something in Alex had changed tonight too. And it wasn't just meeting William's parents that had affected him. She didn't know what. Couldn't pinpoint what it was. But there was a change deep in his soul even more than the difference she'd seen in him after they'd visited the grave.

It wasn't that she only wanted him around for Lilly's sake. Far from it. What she wanted was a chance to make a relationship work with him. A chance to see if they could be together, without William or anything else hanging above them and ruining it before they even started. Without second-guessing themselves.

But it wasn't going to happen. She wouldn't be surprised to wake up in the morning and find him gone.

And it wouldn't just be Lilly hurting if he upped and left. Lisa cared for him. Deeply.

She didn't let her thoughts go any further. Couldn't. Because if she did she'd start wondering if she was in love with him again.

Lisa heard a noise. A creak. She sat bolt upright in bed. Her back so straight it could have snapped.

There was someone in the house.

She crept with stealth from her bed and grabbed the baseball bat tucked in the wardrobe. She glanced out the window. Alex still had his light on. He was awake. She could call to him for help if she needed to.

Lisa moved on tiptoes out into the hall. Her ears strained in the stark silence. The noise below cut a just audible snap through the air.

She moved quietly down the stairs, conscious of the treads to avoid from years of not wanting to wake Lilly when she was young.

A shadow loomed.

"Lisa?"

Her heart fell in a liquid heap to the floor.

"Alex!" She dropped the bat, relieved beyond all measure. "What are you doing in here?"

He didn't answer her.

She could just make him out in the half-light. He had pajama bottoms on. They were slung low, the drawstring tied in a knot.

He walked toward her. His big frame purposeful, determined. Angry?

"Alex?"

He didn't stop. But he did act.

His hand cupped behind her head. His palm filled with her hair. She heard the gasp as it fell from her mouth, but she was powerless to stop it.

Alex's lips found hers before she could even catch her breath. He took her mouth, crushed it into his own, and pulled her hard against his chest.

Her hands found his shoulders, his back, clawed at him to get her body closer to his.

"Alex…" She whispered his name against his skin as he pulled away.

He took one hand from her head and tucked it under her chin. Made her eyes meet his. The other hand was pressed into her lower back, keeping her immobile, forcing her to stay still.

But she didn't need any chains. There was no way her body would move even if her mind told it to.

"I'm sorry."

She opened her mouth to answer, but he pressed his index finger across it to silence her.

"I'm sorry, Lisa. I know now there's nothing I could have done to stop William saving me."

She nodded. His fingers still fell like a clamp across her mouth. He had finally stopped blaming himself. Had released himself. That was the change she'd noticed. His battle with himself over taking this huge step forward was finally done.

"Can we start over?" he asked.

She shook her head.

Confusion made his face crease and gave her the chance to escape him. Just.

"I don't want to start over."

He frowned. His eyes lost the glow they had been casting. His hand fell from her back.

She reached for it and put it in place again. Pulled him against her and let her mouth hover back over his.

"I don't want to start over, Alex. I like you just the way you are."

A smile spread across his face, but she didn't wait to receive it. She caught his bottom lip between both of hers and kissed him, her skin skimming his. She wrapped her arms around him, feeling his muscles, loving the masculinity of his big frame.

Alex scooped her up into his arms, and only then did she let her lips fall from his. She tucked her head against his chest and let herself be carried upstairs to the bedroom.

She had loved William. Wholeheartedly. As much as a wife could love her husband. And now she felt a different but just as powerful surge of love deep within her for Alex. Like her heart had been refilled and she had been given the chance to love all over again. Given the privilege to bask in the glow of another man's feelings toward her without having to give up loving her husband.

Alex looked down at her. He stopped halfway up the stairs.

He kissed her nose, her mouth, then her eyelids as they fluttered shut.

"I love you, Lisa. I love you. *I love you.*"

She tucked tight in against him as he started to walk back up the stairs.

"I love you too," she whispered.

From the thudding of his heart against her ear she could tell he'd heard her.

Lisa woke to light heating her face. She let her eyes pop open, then threw her hand over her eyes. Had she forgotten to close the curtains last night?

She sat up. Last night.

She didn't need to look beside her to know she was in bed alone. There was no weight causing a sag in the mattress. No one's arm had been slung across her when she'd woken. She was alone.

Nausea beat like a drum in her stomach. She reached for her nightdress, discarded on the floor, and wriggled into it before standing. She forced herself to walk to the window.

Had he gone?

She wished upon wishing that he hadn't. But for what other reason would he have disappeared before she woke?

Lisa closed her eyes and felt for the windowframe. She held on to the timber, counted to three, then looked. She didn't know what to expect, but she didn't expect to see Alex.

She placed a hand on the window, the glass cooling her palm and calming her mind.

He was there. With Lilly.

They sat cross-legged on the lawn. They were talking. It looked serious.

Please. *Please.* Don't be telling her that you're going.

She forced herself away from the window and fumbled for

her dressing gown in the wardrobe. She tugged it on and ran fast down the stairs. Her toe caught, but she fought the pain.

He couldn't be leaving.

"Al…" His name died on her lips.

Lilly had run off to chase Boston. She had bare feet and her hair was sticking out around her head, fresh from bed.

"Is she okay?" she gasped.

"She's fine." He got up. A smile tickled the corners of his mouth.

Lisa's own mouth went dry. He was smiling. That was a good thing, right? He walked toward her. She had a flashback to the night before. When he'd stalked her in the same way.

He caught her in his arms and tugged her forward. She resisted. Or tried to.

"Lilly…?"

"Is fine," he said, dropping a kiss to her nose before moving down to her mouth.

Lisa wriggled in protest.

Alex sighed. "I was just telling her something. Something I wanted her to know first."

Lisa tried to pull away from him again, but he held her tight. She was powerless. As good as an insect caught into a spider's web.

"Don't you want to know what I told her?" Alex asked.

She stopped wriggling.

He leaned back, his upper body giving her room but his lower body holding her in place.

She nodded. She wanted to know. Badly.

"You do?" he pressed.

"Yes." She wished her voice wouldn't frog out on her in times of need. It sounded no better than a frog's croak.

"I told her," he said, brushing the hair from her cheek, "that I was going to ask her mommy to marry me. I had to check she was okay with that first, before I did it."

Lisa stared at him. *Marry her?* So he *wasn't* leaving?

"I thought you were going. That you were leaving. That you were telling her…"

Alex stopped her. Covered her mouth with his and kissed the words from her.

"Did you not hear what I told you last night?" he said, when he'd kissed her into stunned silence.

She stared at him. She remembered plenty about last night.

He caught her in his arms, lifting her from her feet and tucking him against her just like he had the night before. "I love you, Lisa." He dropped a kiss on her forehead. "If you'll have me, I want to stay. I'm not going to run. Not now. Not ever. You've taught me that. Made me realize I need to believe in family, in love, in myself again."

She closed her eyes and burrowed into him. Smelt the tangy aftershave that had taunted her from day one. Touched the biceps that had called to her from the first time she'd seen him shirtless. Pulled at the base of his neck to steal a kiss from pillowy lips that had begged to be touching hers from the moment she'd started falling for him.

"So you want to marry me?" She breathed the words against his cheek.

"I thought I was the one who was supposed to ask the question?"

She laughed. A head thrown back, deep in the belly laugh.

"Well, hurry up and ask me so I can say yes," she teased.

He didn't put her down. Just kept her folded in his arms, holding her like he'd never let her go.

A little voice squeaked from behind them.

"Mommy?"

Lisa let Alex swing her around to her daughter. She couldn't wipe the smile off her face if she'd tried.

"Did you say yes?"

Lisa didn't say anything.

He hadn't officially asked her, but of course she would say

yes. How could she not? She loved Alex. As much as she'd loved Lilly's father. So much.

Alex dropped to one knee. He took Lisa's hand.

"I think it's time to make this official. Lisa, will you please put me out of my misery and say you'll marry me?"

"Yes, Mommy. Say yes!" Lilly squealed.

"Yes," whispered Lisa.

Alex stood to wipe away her tears.

"I love you girls, you know?"

"We know," chirped Lilly.

Yes, we know, thought Lisa. And we love you too.

Earlier this year—weeks ago, even—she'd thought her heart would never open to another human being. Hadn't ever wanted it to.

But now she knew otherwise. She loved Alex now, and she'd loved William then—and still did. But her love for William was in the past: a loving, vivid memory to hold on to.

Alex was now.

Alex was her future.

EPILOGUE

ALEX ran his fingers over the emblem lying flat over his chest. The khaki shirt felt nice against his skin. Felt right.

Two months ago he'd been lost. A man without a path. Without a destiny.

Now he was happy. He had a future, and he no longer lay awake at night in a sweat with the world at play on his shoulders.

He tugged on his boots and grabbed the paper bag resting on the counter. He took a peek inside. And smiled. Neatly wrapped sandwiches, a token piece of fruit, and two big slices of cake.

It didn't matter how hard he tried to suppress it, the grin tugging at the corners of his mouth couldn't be stopped.

Alex walked out onto the porch. The lake's water shone in the early-morning light; the trees were waving shadows around the far perimeter. He stood there and looked.

When he was serving, even before that in foster care, he'd never dared to imagine a life like this. A life where everything was possible. Where he had a chance to make his own family, where a woman loved him, and where he could be part of nature every single day.

He walked across the front yard, jingling his keys.

A tap made him look up.

Lisa stood in the window, her hair like a halo framing her face. Lilly was standing in front of her.

His two girls. His two beautiful girls.

He raised a hand and then blew them a slow kiss. His lips brushed his hand before he released it to wave softly up to them.

Lisa pretended to catch it while Lilly giggled. That infectious bubble of laughter that she was so prone to throwing his way.

Alex turned, his hand going up behind him in the air as a final goodbye for the day. He heard the flutter of the flag as it waved proudly in the wind. He didn't have to turn to know it was looking down on him. The same flag that he'd tucked in his bag when he'd first joined the army. It had seen him safely through plenty of hard times, and now it was flying high in the air as a tribute to the friend he'd lost during wartime. A symbol, an ode to William and to how they'd fought over there in the desert. He wanted to show William that he'd take care of Lisa and Lilly until the day he died—just like William had looked out for him at the end.

Alex unlocked the truck and jumped in the cab. Something gave him a feeling that the other National Park ranger would give him a rough time about driving a baby-blue Chevy, but he didn't care.

The rumble of the engine signaled he was on his way.

National Park ranger by day, husband and daddy by night.

Somehow life had finally given him a hand of cards he wanted to play.

He turned up the radio and sang along to the country and western channel Lisa had it permanently dialed to.

He would have preferred rock and roll, but if Lisa wanted country he didn't mind one bit.

Coming Next Month

Available August 9, 2011

You can find more information on upcoming
Harlequin® titles, free excerpts and more at
www.HarlequinInsideRomance.com.

REQUEST YOUR FREE BOOKS!
2 FREE NOVELS PLUS 2 FREE GIFTS!

Harlequin®

Romance

From the Heart, For the Heart

YES! Please send me 2 FREE Harlequin® Romance novels and my 2 FREE gifts (gifts are worth about $10). After receiving them, if I don't wish to receive any more books, I can return the shipping statement marked "cancel". If I don't cancel, I will receive 6 brand-new novels every month and be billed just $4.09 per book in the U.S. or $4.49 per book in Canada. That's a savings of at least 14% off the cover price! It's quite a bargain! Shipping and handling is just 50¢ per book in the U.S. and 75¢ per book in Canada.* I understand that accepting the 2 free books and gifts places me under no obligation to buy anything. I can always return a shipment and cancel at any time. Even if I never buy another book, the two free books and gifts are mine to keep forever.

116/316 HDN FESE

Name _____ (PLEASE PRINT)

Address _____ Apt. #

City _____ State/Prov. _____ Zip/Postal Code

Signature (if under 18, a parent or guardian must sign)

Mail to the **Reader Service:**
IN U.S.A.: P.O. Box 1867, Buffalo, NY 14240-1867
IN CANADA: P.O. Box 609, Fort Erie, Ontario L2A 5X3

Not valid for current subscribers to Harlequin Romance books.

**Are you a subscriber to Harlequin Romance books
and want to receive the larger-print edition?
Call 1-800-873-8635 or visit www.ReaderService.com.**

* Terms and prices subject to change without notice. Prices do not include applicable taxes. Sales tax applicable in N.Y. Canadian residents will be charged applicable taxes. Offer not valid in Quebec. This offer is limited to one order per household. All orders subject to credit approval. Credit or debit balances in a customer's account(s) may be offset by any other outstanding balance owed by or to the customer. Please allow 4 to 6 weeks for delivery. Offer available while quantities last.

Your Privacy—The Reader Service is committed to protecting your privacy. Our Privacy Policy is available online at www.ReaderService.com or upon request from the Reader Service.

We make a portion of our mailing list available to reputable third parties that offer products we believe may interest you. If you prefer that we not exchange your name with third parties, or if you wish to clarify or modify your communication preferences, please visit us at www.ReaderService.com/consumerchoice or write to us at Reader Service Preference Service, P.O. Box 9062, Buffalo, NY 14269. Include your complete name and address.

HRI1B

*Once bitten, twice shy. That's Gabby Wade's motto—
especially when it comes to Adamson men.
And the moment she meets Jon Adamson her theory
is confirmed. But with each encounter a little something
sparks between them, making her wonder if she's been
too hasty to dismiss this one!*

*Enjoy this sneak peek from ONE GOOD REASON
by Sarah Mayberry, available August 2011
from Harlequin® Superromance®.*

Gabby Wade's heartbeat thumped in her ears as she marched
to her office. She wanted to pretend it was because of her
brisk pace returning from the file room, but she wasn't that
good a liar.

Her heart was beating like a tom-tom because Jon Adamson had touched her. In a very male, very possessive way.
She could still feel the heat of his big hand burning through
the seat of her khakis as he'd steadied her on the ladder.

It had taken every ounce of self-control to tell him to
unhand her. What she'd really wanted was to grab him by
his shirt and, well, explore all those urges his touch had
instantly brought to life.

While she might not like him, she was wise enough to
understand that it wasn't always about liking the other person. Sometimes it was about pure animal attraction.

Refusing to think about it, she turned to work. When
she'd typed in the wrong figures three times, Gabby admitted she was too tired and too distracted. Time to call it a
day.

As she was leaving, she spied Jon at his workbench in
the shop. His head was propped on his hand as he studied
blueprints. It wasn't until she got closer that she saw his

eyes were shut.

He looked oddly boyish. There was something innocent and unguarded in his expression. She felt a weakening in her resistance to him.

"Jon." She put her hand on his shoulder, intending to shake him awake. Instead, it rested there like a caress.

His eyes snapped open.

"You were asleep."

"No, I was, uh, visualizing something on this design." He gestured to the blueprint in front of him then rubbed his eyes.

That gesture dealt a bigger blow to her resistance. She realized it wasn't only animal attraction pulling them together. She took a step backward as if to get away from the knowledge.

She cleared her throat. "I'm heading off now."

He gave her a smile, and she could see his exhaustion.

"Yeah, I should, too." He stood and stretched. The hem of his T-shirt rose as he arched his back and she caught a flash of hard male belly. She looked away, but it was too late. Her mind had committed the image to permanent memory.

And suddenly she knew, for good or bad, she'd never look at Jon the same way again.

Find out what happens next in ONE GOOD REASON, available August 2011 from Harlequin® Superromance®!

Celebrating

Blaze™ **10** *years of* red-hot reads

Featuring a special August author lineup of
six fan-favorite authors who have written
for Blaze™ from the beginning!

The Original Sexy Six:

Vicki Lewis Thompson

Tori Carrington

Kimberly Raye

Debbi Rawlins

Julie Leto

Jo Leigh

Pick up all six Blaze™
Special Collectors' Edition titles!

August 2011

Plus visit
HarlequinInsideRomance.com
and click on the Series Excitement Tab
for exclusive Blaze™ 10th Anniversary content!